Apocrypha is a Sin Eater, a mercenary who does all the jobs the corporations do not want anybody to know about that need to get done. She is an experienced operative who thought she had seen it all, but this time, she is up against cyborgs, elves, and the undead, all the while trying to break in a new partner. The stakes have never been higher, because if she doesn't complete the mission, her father will pay the ultimate price.

SIN EATERS

APOCRYPHA, BOOK ONE

KATHRYNE LENTES

A NineStar Press Publication
www.ninestarpress.com

Sin Eaters

First Edition, May 2025
ISBN: 978-1-64890-870-5
Also available in eBook, ISBN: 978-1-64890-869-9

CONTENT WARNING:
This book contains the death of a minor character, gore, graphic violence, and guns.

This book is dedicated to my son and spouse who make living livable and gave me all the love and support I needed to make this book a reality.

"Long is the way and hard, that out of Hell leads up to light."

> — *John Milton, Paradise Lost*

I'm the new messiah

Death Angel with a gun

Dangerous in my silence

Deadly to my cause.

> —*Speak, song by Queensrÿche, Written by Geoff Tate/Michael Wilton*

Prologue

The young woman looked at the growing crowd of children; they had come back every day and brought more friends each time. Some liked her stories, some just wanted to be part of the group, and a select few listened and were getting close to understanding. Not too close, she hoped; she knew what came from complete understanding and wanted to let them enjoy their youth more than she had.

"Any questions before we start today?"

"What's your name?"

"How did you get in here?"

"Why is your hair so many colors?"

"Will you go out with me?" That one was new; she must have started attracting an older audience without noticing it.

She thought about the questions. She had not given a name at these events yet and hesitated. She had gone by many names, some inappropriate in this setting. Crossroads thought about using the name she had been given by her parents, but she couldn't; that was all she had left from them, and she could not share it. She thought about where her life had begun and said, "Crossroads."

"Crossroads—that's a stupid name."

She glared at the child in the front row, and he closed his mouth. She continued, "My stage name is Crossroads; you know, like a band has a name they perform under. How I got here... Well, there are not many places I can't go if I put my mind to it. As to the hair, well, that is a long story, and I am not dating anyone now, no matter how cute they are." She finished with a wink toward the teenager in the back row. That should give him some points with his classmates for a day or two. "I have come here to tell you a story. The story is of this world and how it got to be the way it is."

"We know that story. Our teachers taught us that." Another look at the kid in the front row; she was starting to think he was going to be trouble.

"And what did they tell you?"

"The aliens came and destroyed the world, and only the people who were safe in the biospheres survived. That's us; everybody else is dead or has turned into a monster."

"That is an interesting story, and I am sure they would not lie to you, but let me tell you a different story. If you don't believe me, then just remember it as a fantasy to think about when you are daydreaming."

She put down the guitar she had been idly tuning while she spoke and stood up. She was tall for a woman at five-ten, and many years of performing had taught her to have a commanding presence, and the children quieted down as they approached the center of the makeshift stage. She pulled back her long rainbow-tinted hair and twirled it into a bun with a pencil, a trick she had learned from her mother, who had been a librarian of sorts.

"The world has not always been as it is. That statement is true of almost any age, as Dickens said." This time, she froze the child in the front row before he could ask who Dickens was. "But times do not usually change as quickly as they did in the last ten years. Your parents created this place before the time of change. They thought the world was going to hell and wanted to divorce themselves from the outside. Then came the visitors, the aliens as you call them, and as they say, all bets were off. The war was terrible and cost more lives than most people can count. It also made a shift in the very laws that people thought regulated the world. The visitors had highly advanced technology and weapons that seemed to be more powerful than imagined. They rained destruction on the world, took thousands of people hostage, and performed experiments on them to see the range of our genetic code. They were amazed at what potential we had within us; just as it is almost impossible to see that a wolf and a poodle are cousins, so you could not look at many of these people and recognize them as human. This was the first mistake they made because many of these Cybreds, as they were to be called, broke free and fought the invaders with their newfound abilities.

"Your parents were not the only ones who fled the cities. There was a mass exodus to places of worship and sanctuary; the Vatican, Stonehenge, Cahokia Mounds, and the Masjid al-Haram all were soon surrounded by teeming masses seeking solace in the old ways to save them. The visitors thought these were military enclaves and sent fire from the sky to consume them. Then a strange thing happened; there were some deaths but not as many as there should have been. The holy places seemed to take in the energy, and the ley lines erupted." She made no face at the kid in front; she wanted him to ask the question.

"There's no such thing as a ley line. You made that up?"

"Have your teachers taught you about latitude and longitude, lines drawn around the world that sailors of old used to navigate the globe? Ley lines are the lines of power surrounding the earth, but they hold the life force of that planet; they hold its magic. The power of the weapons filled the lines, and they erupted, spilling out the magic they held and creating the Manna Sphere. A source of energy that the strong-willed and skilled could manipulate..."

A host of children started to open their mouths at this but stopped as a glowing nimbus of energy appeared over her outstretched palm. It widened and opened to seemingly become a hole in the air, a hole that appeared to lead to somewhere...elsewhere.

"The power does not just exist in an active state. It also affects things passively. Changelings have started to appear, babies born to normal parents whose appearance and abilities match those of races thought extinct or just a product of myth and legend. It also had an effect on diseases, creating new ones that rob a person of all semblances of life save the hunger for flesh. These diseases have consumed the country of Australia and there the world is just as your teachers describe it. But there are other places such as England, which has become a new home for all changelings and where magic has transformed it."

The children listened intently, and their eyes were fixated on the sphere, which showed scenes corresponding to the vistas she told them of.

"Not all people are so accepting of the new things. Europe has banned either changelings or Cybreds from having any form of citizenship. America is a divided place; some people live in biospheres like you do, cutting themselves off from any outside contact, while others embrace the new frontiers we have been shown.

Some parts of America have even greatly benefited from the Manna Sphere, such as the Alliance of Tribes, who have taken back parts of the lands they once lived on. The other people who have gained are the criminal element who were swift to bring those with dark gifts into their organization. Now they truly deserve the name the underworld."

Some of the children had begun to back up as the visions in the sphere turned dark.

"The world is not all safe and quiet. I would be a fool to tell you it is, but I am letting you know that you have a choice between what you have and what you could have."

The portal winked out of existence and the children snapped out of their reverie. A moment later, a terrible shouting came from the back of the crowd. Five men in long gray dusters that marked them as Pilgrims, the law enforcement arm of the biosphere corporation, yelled at the children to disperse as they moved toward Crossroads.

"Took you long enough, guys. Minneapolis found me in three days, and it took you guys a whole week."

*

Crossroads sat in the steel-back chair in the same gray room she had sat in a score of times before. She kept hoping that someone would paint these differently. They could have tried black instead of gray or maybe dark blue. She knew all the biospheres were constructed from the same plans, but she hoped someone, somewhere would display some creativity. Though that wasn't the purpose of the spheres; security was, at any cost.

Exactly twenty-five minutes later, the supervisor slammed into the room while the second-in-command strolled languidly behind them.

"Who the hell are you?"

If you had gotten to my show a little earlier, you would have caught the introduction. "I'm Crossroads. Well, that is more like my nom de plume, but that's all you are going to get. And I bet you're pissed because my fingerprints did not come up in the federal banks, nor did the DNA come up in the Mormon records. Now you're wondering, if I'm not on the grid, how did I get through the front door?"

The supervisor backhanded Crossroads, and she went to the floor. Then the subordinate helped her up. She wondered if the slap was in the textbook or if she just brought that out in authority figures.

"You're not helping yourself out."

"Actually, that is exactly what I am doing. You can play dumb, but I checked out your gates, and they have magic and tech security measures, so you know what you're doing. And if you know what you're doing, then you know what's coming. I'm just trying to make sure the huddled masses have a clue, and maybe one or two of them grow up to be of use in the coming fight." She laid the handcuffs they had placed her in on the table in front of her. "Now I have a performance in Seattle that I have to get ready for. TTFN." She stood up and made a gesture at the mirrored surface on the wall, and it grew translucent. A moment later, she dived through it and was gone.

Chapter One

Apocrypha was in the hospital again. She closed her eyes for a moment and drank in her surroundings, which were at once so familiar yet disquieting. The smell of antiseptic, the sound of the nurses' conversation at the front desk, the echoing cries of people who had given up on using the call button, the feel of the vinyl armrests of the chair, so close to comfortable. She released her breath and opened her eyes. Her father was silent as he had been for two days, the only indication he was still with her being the rising and falling of his chest and the regular beeping of the machines monitoring his condition. She gripped the handles of the chair as the machines briefly changed their syncopation. Still, a moment later, they returned to their gentle pattern.

She rose to her feet, her hands moving across her body to check on her phone and keys. Then, she adjusted the shoulder rig that held her gun and went to the window. The doctor had said he would be there in the morning to discuss her father's illness, but it was now almost 12:30, and she was swiftly running out of patience. The window showed nothing but the large expanse of the hospital's parking garage, a view she had long since memorized. She turned around as several people entered the room. Her father's roommate had a steady stream of people moving in and out. She wondered what it would be like to have a large family; for as long as she could remember, it had only been her and her father. She sat back down in the chair and waited.

Three hours later, the doctor walked in.

"Hi, I am Doctor Studivant." The doctor handed her his card. She looked at it briefly and slid it into her back pocket to join the ten or so other doctors' business cards she already possessed. She shook his hand and smiled. She had long ago stopped getting upset at the doctors showing up late; it was part of her life, like being shot at.

"Is there any news about my father?"

"Well, your father's condition is complicated. We are not just dealing with a normal disease. The influenza is manna-infused and actively disrupts any drugs we try to use. I have never seen anything like it except in journals. His reports say he spent a lot of time out of the country."

"We traveled a lot as missionaries in the past, but we have been in the city for the last couple of years."

"What can happen is that a person can catch the disease in an area without magic, and then once the patient enters an area with more magic present, it can feed off that power and use it to attack the carrier."

The doctor stopped for a minute, and his face slid into a carefully constructed expression, giving away no emotions. Apocrypha knew that face. It meant bad news was coming.

"The problem is that while we can treat the symptoms he is

experiencing and keep his vital functions going, we do not have the ability to fight the root cause. I am not sure of your religious views, but have you contacted The Word? They have bishops who are capable healers and might be able to purge the infection from your father."

"My father has certain...objections to the church. Are there any other options?"

The doctor looked around the room, not meeting her eyes.

"Listen, doctor, I am open to anything that might help him."

"I do know some people who provide alternate care, but they are not licensed and highly expensive."

"Just give me their names and I will go from there."

Apocrypha looked at her dad in the hospital bed one last time and walked out of the room. After listening to the doctor's prognosis, she knew she was going to need cash to fix this. Black market shamans were never cheap and rarely dependable, but her family would never go to The Word for help. She pulled out her phone and hit the first speed dial.

"Sin Eaters corporate resolution solutions. How may I help you?"

"Marie, this is Apocrypha, is Vince around?"

"He's not in."

"Is he not in or not taking my phone call?"

"...um...well."

"It's okay, Marie. I shouldn't have put you on the spot. Just let him know I called and am open to any assignment he might have for me, dungeon crawl included."

"I will."

Apocrypha closed the phone, took a few steps away, then turned back, balling up her fist to smash the wall. She stopped the punch one inch from the wall. The last thing she needed was for her dad to be removed from the hospital because she got violent. She should go back into the room and hold her dad's hand. That would be what her mom would have done, but she couldn't take his unresponsiveness and fled out of the door. She jumped onto her motorcycle, a fully customized Lady Shiva. She revved up the engine, knowing she would have to sell it soon if she did not get a job. The bike steered itself through the streets for several hours, and eventually, she found herself in front of an old church.

Apocrypha slipped quietly into the church. She found a place at the end of the pew all the way in the back and sat down. She pulled her hooded sweatshirt closer around her head, tucking in the edges of her long white hair, which was trying to escape. It was late at night, and the building was largely empty. The cathedral had once been part of the Catholic church but had been repurposed and expanded into one of the bustling mega-parishes of the Church of the Word.

The Word, as most people referred to it now, had risen to prominence during the great conflict when man learned that he was not alone in the universe. The ten-year war had changed many things in the world, including magic returning to the globe and the reintegration of most Christian sects into the Catholic Church. The Church of the Word was an attempt to bring the Christian religion back to the forefront like it had been in the Middle Ages. The new church offered people relief from the disasters of the great conflict through traditional means, and it did not hurt that many of the heads of the church could now perform actual miracles. Gone were all the small churches of the different denominations. They were replaced by grand edifices holding thousands of believers, but within some of them were the same priests who tended the flock before everything had changed.

Father Raphael was one of them. He stood at one of the

microphones, his graying hair barely covering his head as he practiced a sermon he would be giving on Sunday. He made a sweeping gesture with his hand to illustrate a point and caught sight of Apocrypha. She locked eyes with him, then looked over at the confessional booth.

He nodded his head and gathered up his sermon materials. Apocrypha stood up and pulled the back of her sweatshirt down to make sure the gun she had stuffed in her waistband would not become visible. She walked into the confessional and kneeled. After a moment, Father Raphael opened the divider separating them.

"Greetings, Apocrypha..." Father Raphael sighed loudly. "Do I really have to call you that? It's not who you are; it's just some headhunter persona you wear on the streets."

"It's who I am now. Who I must be, and I need to always stay focused."

"You have other options."

"No, no, I don't. With all due respect, Father, I came for penance, not for career counseling."

"Fine, how long has it been since your last confession?"

"A couple months." Apocrypha waited to be admonished, but Father Raphael merely continued the ceremony.

"Announce your sins so that you may receive absolution."

"I miss the Latin."

"So do I, but we give up a little ceremony to reach more people. Besides, you can't be old enough to remember when services were in Latin."

"My first church was what you call old school."

"Really..." Father Raphael waited for a long moment to see if Apocrypha would share, but only silence answered him. He decided to continue with the sacrament. "What are your transgressions?"

"I have borne false witness. I have harbored lustful thoughts. I have sworn and taken the lord's name in vain."

"And how many have you assaulted this week while performing your job duties?"

"I don't count that as a sin."

"You are going to tell me what constitutes a sin?"

"Well, they were all bad people; besides, it was for their own good."

"Please enlighten me."

"I had to gain entry to someplace I should not have been..."

"Which you also failed to count among your sins."

"...and if I were to go in like a ninja, then the guards are punished for not doing their job. If I smack some people around, then they get to keep their job, plus they get worker's compensation, so it's for the best if I assault them."

"That might be true, but you like smacking them, which turns it into a sin."

"Okay, I assaulted about twenty-seven people."

"And..." Father Raphael let the silence linger for a moment, which he usually did when making a point. "That is not why you are here today. This is an unscheduled visit. I know if you had to confess every time you smacked someone, I would have to install a drive-through window."

"I have been unfaithful to a person who I considered family, and because of my actions, my father is now going to suffer."

"That does not sound like you. You are many things, but unfaithful is not one of them."

"How would you know what I am really like?"

"How do you kids say it? This is not my first rodeo. I have learned a lot about judging character and, your choice of occupation notwithstanding, I believe you to be a good soul."

"I once believed that, Father, but the choices we make drive us down bitter paths, and sometimes I can't even remember the person I used to be. A friend labeled me as a betrayer and cut me off from their life."

"Tell me the whole story, my child."

"I was working. It was a simple job recovering a hard drive full of pharmaceutical data from a rival corp that had stolen it. Me and my partner Novembre went in. We overcame the resistance and penetrated the facility."

"So, you broke in and assaulted their guards."

"Yes. We got into the lab, and they were already starting to produce the drugs. I prepared to destroy the product while Novembre checked the data. It turned out the drug was a treatment for Achilles Syndrome. The corporation apparently had one for several months and not released it to the public. Novembre said we had a duty to give the information to clinics, but we were under contract to return the hard drive to the company."

"Novembre does not sound like a usual headhunter."

"She's not. She had some trouble with the law, and I convinced Vince to put up bail for her in exchange for her doing work for us. We had history. She helped me when I first came to St. Louis. We had run the streets for a while before I got recruited for Sin Eaters. She was never comfortable with the arrangement but signed up because she trusted me that we would not do the really dirty jobs."

"So, what happened?"

"When she saw that I wasn't going to go for it, she tried to cast a spell. She was a major league mage, but those things take a little time to generate. I decked her before she could. Now she hates me; Vince didn't pay me for the gig and has been slow in giving me a new assignment. Which means I don't have the money to pay for the care my father needs. Am I being punished by Him for my choices?"

"My child..."

Apocrypha continued before he could finish his sentence," I am not a bad person. I have done things I had thought I never would; I do retrievals, I do protection, I do dungeon crawls, but I don't do assassination or interrogation, and when I give my word on something, I follow through."

"My child, I do not think you are a bad person. It is a harsh world with difficult choices. I am confused as to why your boss wants to fire you."

"Well, he thinks I should have brought Novembre back in cuffs since he put up the bail bond money. Also, the client was concerned that all the samples made by the rival corporation might not have been destroyed. Apparently, Novembre was able to hide some in her pouch before I knocked her out. I guess the clinic she woke up at was able to replicate some of the materials and get it to people in need."

"Novembre stuck them in her pouch?"

"She was always sneaky."

"Apocrypha, I absolve you of your sins; for penance, I prescribe you to stop being so hard on yourself. God does hold us responsible for our choices, but I don't believe He is punishing you. Maybe he is just trying to nudge you into a different career. I also suggest that whatever your objections, you avail yourself of our services for your father's care, but I know you will not. I suggest you pray over your circumstances and do what you feel is God's plan for you. Go and sin no more."

"Thank you, Father." Apocrypha closed her eyes; she had not believed in God's plans for a long time. She thought of him more like an absent watchman or a man who set the chess pieces up before her but never bothered to teach her the rules. She wasn't going to tell Father Raphael that. She also did not feel like thoughtful prayer; she felt like getting drunk or kicking somebody's ass. She did know one place where she could probably arrange both.

Chapter Two

Caliber Cats was an unusual mix of bar, cat café, and pawn store. It was the only place in Saint Louis that let you drink or buy guns twenty-four hours a day while also playing with cats. She grabbed a stool at the end of the bar and looked at the wide assortment of bottles and firearms adorning the walls while a large calico walked across the bar in front of her. She tapped on the bar and entered her customer code into the display that popped up; a moment later, a Budweiser rose out of the bar. Apocrypha popped the tab, wrapped her hands around it to put it to her lips, and stopped.

"If you put your hand on me without permission, you'll lose it." She swiveled around on the stool; standing before her was a lanky man wearing a Hawaiian shirt covered in kittens and a pair of enormous handguns.

"How is it you always know?"

"Trade secret, Woody, you know how it goes."

"Not anymore, I retired from that life. Also, don't call me that; people around here call me Mr. Wood. I can't believe I got drunk enough to tell you about my nickname from basic. That is one of the many reasons I stopped drinking. Anyway, now I just pass out the guns and let you kids have all the fun." Mr. Wood put a box on top of the bar. "I figure you are here for the usual."

"Yeah...sure." Apocrypha started pulling out guns and knives and placing them in the box. She did not have a job pending, but she should be prepared in case Vince changed his mind.

"I still don't get why you replace all your guns after every op."

"Just a superstition. It's like baseball; you got to respect the streak."

"If you say so. Your superstition puts more money in my pocket, but I feel a little bad about taking the cash from you. I heard you got stiffed for that last job."

"Wow, that got around the neighborhood fast. You feel bad enough to not charge me?"

"Not that bad."

Apocrypha watched as Mr. Wood picked up the box. She did not share the fact that she was getting rid of them because a skilled mage could track you by items that you carried on your person for extended periods of time and, given the person who told her that might be tracking her right now, she did not think it was time to break the habit. "You are destroying those and not reselling them, right?"

"Scouts' honor."

Apocrypha turned her head sideways and gave him a doubting look. Mr. Wood held up three fingers in the Boy Scout salute.

"I was really, back in the day when we still had Boy Scouts. So, besides replacement guns, can I get you anything? I have an excellent selection of plastic explosives that just came in."

"No thanks on the boom-boom, but I am looking for any kind of work."

"I don't know of anything paying at the moment, but I will keep an ear open."

"Is there anything out there not paying but a good cause? I need to work out a bad mood, and smacking somebody who deserves it would be a good start."

"Not much. I mean, there is the auction, but you don't want to mess around with that." Mr. Wood motioned to a towering minotaur who was passing by and handed him the box. "Throw those in the grinder."

"Auction?" Apocrypha took a long drag from the beer.

"There is a new group of crazies who just moved into town. They call themselves the Purifiers. They believe in humanity first; think the KKK, but for changelings. They want to wipe out anything magical or non-human in America."

"And they have auctions?"

"They like to round up young nubile changelings, elves, dryads, nymphs, etc., etc., and sell them off to the highest bidder. They have converted the old racetrack into an encampment."

"And no one has done anything about this."

"Well, the authorities keep condemning it, but it's across the river, which means the corps don't care. They are also heavily armed, so the local cops don't stand a chance."

"Well then." Apocrypha finished what was left of her beer in one drink and placed it back on the bar. "Why don't you get me my replacements, and I will go pay them a visit."

"I would not do that; these guys are serious. They built up the track to be a mini fortress, and they have a small army at the front entrance that makes sure nobody goes in packing. It's not a one-person run."

"You're right. I need some backup. Get me some of those plastic explosives and an extra set of pistols."

Mr. Wood held up his hands. "Okay, I don't want to know anymore. Just don't get yourself killed. I might miss you."

"Miss me or my credits?"

Mr. Wood just smiled and walked away.

Apocrypha watched as he left. That was the usual rule of the street: you might like other people, but you were on your own at the end of the day. She had forgotten that working with Novembre, and she hoped it had not cost her the edge she needed.

Apocrypha made a couple of extra stops, picking up her ballistic-resistant duster and some other gear, then got back on her motorcycle. She ran her hands over the seat's leather as she got on. The Lady Shiva was the top of the Tractdyne motorcycle line and had been given as a rare bonus from Vince for completing a job. She had demanded a little something extra after almost being impregnated with eggs by a mutated spider the size of a Buick. She shuddered at the memory. She really hated dungeon crawls.

The drive was uneventful, and she parked several blocks away and paid a local gang to keep an eye on her bike. She pulled her dagger from the scabbard on her gun belt and slid it in her boot as she covered the distance to the main gate. The auction was well in swing by the time she got there. A squad of twenty heavily armed men was at the gate, taking guns and placing them in a nearby bunker. She rolled up her ammo belt with her weapons in their holsters. She handed them to the biggest, most tattooed individual she had ever seen. He looked her up and down, taking a long time with his eyes fixated on her breasts, then finally gave her a metal chit. The second biggest thug ran a metal detector over her. She raised her hand with her cell phone as they passed the wand. The wand ran over her boot without a single noise. She smiled and walked in, glad that her knife, Thorn, did not register as metal on any scanner. The blade had been in her family for more generations than she could count and was a reliquary. She was unsure what holy item had been placed in it when it was forged. Still, it had cut through almost any substance she had ever tried it against, except for ordinary human flesh, and was anathema to demons and the undead.

She entered the compound and made her way into what was once the speedway. She sauntered through the crowd, taking note that the Purifiers who were walking around were armed only with knives and clubs. They must have been confident that no one would get through the checkpoint with a firearm. They had built a sizeable wooden dais in the middle of what was once the racetrack. A guy with a purple mohawk that reminded her of Novembre's was extorting the group to bid more for a young wood nymph who was in chains. Apocrypha jumped over the bottom of the stands and started walking toward the center. The guy with the mohawk yelled at some of his fellows to stop her.

Apocrypha pulled off her duster, swirled it around her head, and threw it to the ground. Then, she pulled her sweatshirt over her head, revealing a tight tank top that showed she was not wearing a bra. She wrapped the sleeves of the sweatshirt around her waist as she walked. The head Purifier waved off his compatriots and started yelling for her to keep going. She started running and advanced up the stairs and dropped to her knees.

"Our Father who art in heaven." She began to pray.

"Oh, what the hell. I thought you were a party girl."

Apocrypha kept her head down. "Hallowed be thy name."

The crowd started booing and jeering as she continued.

The guy with the mohawk had had enough and jabbed Apocrypha's shoulder with the top of a baseball bat with spikes driven through it. "You're hot, babe; too bad you're crazy. Now get the fuck off my stage."

"And deliver us from evil..." As Apocrypha finished her prayer, she clicked the button on the side of her phone, and a massive explosion rocked the stadium. The plastic explosives she had stuffed into the pistols she had given the guards had set off all the ammunition stored in the bunker. The guy with the mohawk screamed, and Apocrypha rose to her feet, grabbing the end of his bat as she stood. She twisted it from his hand. She flipped the bat in the air, caught it by the grip, and smashed the Purifier in the face. He hurtled from the stage in an eruption of blood. The crowd that had gathered for the auction was yelling and running in complete disorder. Apocrypha allowed herself a smile then clamped down on her emotions as more Purifiers rushed her.

She caught the first as he topped the steps with a spinning back-kick, sending him flying off to the side. The second one had a machete, and she parried his overhead cut with the bat and kicked him in the gut, driving him back into the other assailant.

"Look out," the wood nymph yelled, and Apocrypha spun around to see a Purifier sprinting at her from the other side with a Bowie knife. She reacted instinctively and threw the bat and impaled the Purifier, and he went down.

Apocrypha dropped to her knees and pulled her dagger from her boot. She slashed at the chains holding the nymph and the blade sliced through the metal like a hot knife through butter.

"Where are the other captives?"

"In the old pit area." The wood nymph pointed to the far side of the track.

"Okay, let's go get them."

The wood nymph's face went white. "I have to get out of here."

"And we will, all of us together. What is your name?"

"Diana."

"Okay, Diana." Apocrypha pressed the knife into the wood nymph's hand. "You take this and cut them free, and I will protect you. Can you do that?"

"Yeah, I think so."

"Then let's go."

Apocrypha got back up and turned to the steps. The two Purifiers she had knocked down had recovered and were coming back up. Apocrypha twisted her neck to either side and cracked her knuckles. She was more than most people saw, and on an average run, she had to hold back. She wasn't going to accidentally kill some rent-a-cop just trying to pay his mortgage, but these guys... These guys were different; she could enjoy this.

The guy with the machete came at her first, and she caught his wrist as he brought the blade down. She took a grip and applied pressure, grinding the small bones together. He cried out in pain and dropped the weapon; maintaining her grip, she spun him around and threw him into the other rushing attacker. They landed hard in a heap at the bottom of the stairs and did not move.

Apocrypha descended the steps, taking them two at a time and dragging Diana behind her. The Purifier camp was in utter chaos, and people ran everywhere, unsure of what was happening. Because of this, they could get across the pits without further entanglement. The pits once used to refuel the racecars had been converted into a series of cages. As they approached, a hulking figure stepped out of the shadows of the cages. The man was almost six-seven, was heavily muscled, and had had his arms replaced with glittering chrome cybernetics.

Apocrypha skidded to a stop. "Okay, so that's no to changelings, but yes to steroids and cyborgs, got it." She motioned to

Diana. "Start opening the pens. I will handle this guy."

"Yeah, good luck with that."

The cyborg looked at Apocrypha and smiled a wide, toothless grin.

"Really, you spent thousands on cybernetic limbs and could not buck up to fix the meth mouth."

The cyborg surged forward faster than Apocrypha would have thought possible and smashed his fist into her face. She spun around, trying to roll with the punch, but the force still drove her to the ground. She shook her head to clear the stars from her vision. Before she could recover, the cyborg grabbed her around the neck with both hands and lifted her into the air. The metal hands clamped tightly on her throat, cutting off her breath. She beat on the arms repeatedly, but they were unyielding. She clawed at the air, trying to reach the brute's face, but it was out of her reach. Darkness started to intrude on her vision, and she reached for the only thing she could on the bare-chested cyborg. She grabbed his nipples and twisted and twisted till they ripped from his chest, and he dropped her, clutching his chest in pain.

Apocrypha hit the ground, too dazed to do anything to soften the impact. She took a deep breath, refilling her lungs with oxygen. She got to her hands and knees, but before she could stand up, the brute was upon her again, kicking her in the gut. She was sent sprawling back to the ground. The cyborg slammed its arm down into her neck again, pinning her to the ground, and reared its other arm back. Apocrypha closed her eyes, knowing that blow would end this. A long second passed without the strike and Apocrypha opened her eyes to see four changelings holding on to the cyborg's arm. They would not be able to stall him for long.

"Hey, lady," Diana cried out, and she threw the dagger back toward Apocrypha. The dagger landed back in her grip, and she lashed out, severing the cyborg's hand at the wrist. She regained her footing, braced herself, and threw a punch with all her strength directly into his throat. The brute stagged back and gurgled for a moment, then fell to the ground, choking on his own blood. Apocrypha took a deep breath and wondered if maybe it was time to find a career counselor.

Chapter Three

"I can't believe you're abandoning me."

Kitsune ran her hands through her blue hair. She took a deep breath and turned to face her mother.

"I am not abandoning you. I have set things up with the bank; you will get a monthly deposit of two thousand dollars, more than enough to cover rent, food, and whatever Harold can drink."

"You keep your mouth shut about Harold. He loves me, unlike some people."

Kitsune dropped to one knee next to the kitchen table. "I love you, but I can't stay here. Things are changing, and not for the better. I need to make a fresh start."

"Oh, your computer hobby."

"It's not a hobby." Kitsune took another deep breath.

"And why do you have to start it in Saint Louis? Are you too good for Detroit?"

"I have to leave Detroit because as long as I am here, the

people I used to work for will always try to pull me back in. It was one thing when the term underworld was a metaphor, but now most of the family is getting deeper in bed with dark magic, and it's not going to end well."

"So, you're just going to leave me to their mercy."

"They won't do that. Me and the Don have enough on each other that we would..."

"The Don and I... I taught you to speak correctly."

Kitsune smacked her head against the kitchen table. "The Don and I have enough dirt on each other that it makes no sense for either of us to cross the other. He is not going to be happy, but he won't take any action against you."

"Says you."

Kitsune got to her feet. "Mom, I got to go. If you need to call me, make sure to use that burner phone; I got you." She pulled her duffel bag off the floor and made her way to the door. She turned the knob and started to walk out.

"I am sorry I made you do it."

"I know, Mom." Kitsune closed the door behind her.

*

Kitsune flopped down into the seat of the bus and dropped her bag into the seat next to her. The trip to St Louis would be a long drive, but she had work to do, and it was one of the least traceable ways to travel. She waited until the bus pulled out of the station and got out her tablet. She called up a file on her first mark in the city, Vince Davidson. She slowly flipped through documents on her screen. He was the head of Sin Eater Associates, one of the first headhunter groups to come into being.

"Wait a second, what is a sin-eater?" She quickly pulled up a new tab on her browser.

A sin-eater is a person who consumes a ritual meal in order to spiritually take on the sins of a deceased person. The food was believed to absorb the sins of a recently dead person, thus absolving the soul of the person. Cultural anthropologists and folklorists classify sin-eating as a form of ritual. It is most commonly associated with Scotland, Ireland, Wales, English counties bordering Wales, and Welsh culture.

"I guess that makes sense for a mercenary group that is paid to do other people's dirty jobs," she mumbled to herself and returned to her other research.

They had started as a group of moderately successful military contractors in the early 2000s but really grew to prominence after the invasion by allowing changelings and Cybreds into their forces. The group had initially been formed of three people: Vince, his father Warren, and their partner Jamison Winters, who was a former colonel in the army. Jamison had brought the military knowledge, and the Davidsons had brought the money. The group had fallen on tough times recently. Jameson had been killed a year ago when an op went bad, and Warren had died of a heart attack. Vince responded by coming up with the determination system. In the world of headhunters, it was common to have customers in many of the major corporations, and the people you were raiding this week might be the ones you were guarding next. So, Vince had begun offering existing customers the option to pay him not to make a run against their organization. He would tell them the money he was offered but not the job, and if they matched the offer, he would turn down the job. This allowed him a steady stream of revenue without having to work for it. He also started what was called Vince's Rule Number One. The rule was *if the money is there, we do not care.*

"Vince would probably fit in with my old employer pretty well," Kitsune muttered to herself. She then flicked through the documents and pulled up the most recent one. It was a copy of an industry magazine article exhorting the benefits of using headhunters. It had a picture of the Saligia Corporation's head of security, Vlad Mathern, with his arm around Vince. She quickly went through the article one more time, then hit a phone program on her tablet to change the number that showed up on caller ID to that of Saligia.

"Sin Eaters Associates, this is Marie; how can I help you?"

"Marie, hi, this is Janice from Saligia Corporate Relations."

"Yes, Janice, I will get Vince on the phone right away."

"No, don't do that just yet. We at Saligia are delighted with the ways you guys have come through for us lately and wanted to showcase our gratitude by offering Vince some companionship. But we want it to be off the book and in a subtle manner. Would you happen to know what his favorite bar is and, for lack of a better term, his type?"

"I am not sure I have that information."

"Hey, if it's an uncomfortable situation, I will just tell Mr. Mathern that Vince isn't interested in enjoying our gifts. I am sure he will not be insulted by a refusal of his generosity."

"No, I did not mean to imply that. Vince likes to hit Blueberry Hill in the loop on Friday nights. As for a type, he likes them—well, young, blonde, and dumb."

"Don't all men. Well, thanks for the information, and please don't tell Vince. We would like it to be a surprise."

"Okay, and oh, one more thing, if you really want to get into his good graces, I know you guys are launching that new simulated intelligence program, Virtual Companion Five. Vince would kill to be in the beta test for that."

"I will see what I can do."

Kitsune clicked the icon and terminated the call. She then pulled up a directory of high-class escort services and hit the connection on the one that seemed the most upscale.

"Seductive Services, this is Veronica, how can we help you?"

Kitsune took a moment to ponder the fact that a mercenary service and a brothel both answered their phones the same way. "I was looking to hire a young lady to provide a night's entertainment to a friend of mine."

"What did you have in mind? The more specific you can be, the better services we can provide.'

"Um, a twentysomething hot blonde, meet at a bar and have him think he picked her up, probably spend the night but nothing kinky."

"If the parameters of the engagement change, the fee will be increased substantially."

Kitsune gritted her teeth for a moment. She probably should have researched Vince's predilections, but maybe he would save the weird stuff for the second date. "I understand."

"Well, for a standard Alpha overnight engagement, the fee will be fifteen hundred."

"Really." Kitsune whistled softly; that was almost everything she had put aside after setting up her mom. But this mission had to be successful. "Okay, yeah, sounds good."

"Okay, as soon as the payment clears, I will email you the escort's contact information, and you can give her the details."

"Thanks."

"No, thank you, and we hope to be able to service you again in the near future."

Kitsune hit the digital hang-up. She tapped her fingers and looked out of the window of the bus while she thought of the next step in her plan. She needed a way into Vince's systems, and Vince's assistant might have given her one. She pulled up her connection to the net and zipped to Cutthroat Bay. The site was the home of every illegal download in the world, and it took her only a few minutes of searching to find a beta copy of Virtual Companion. While she was downloading the items, the email from Seductive Services came with details of Vince's date, Betty. The file included a variety of pictures of Betty clad and unclad. Kitsune was impressed and wondered if Betty was available for dates with either gender. She pushed that thought aside. She would never be able to afford her.

Once the files for the virtual companion program were downloaded, she took a couple of hours to insert Betty's pictures into the files, then shut down her computer. She leaned back against the window and let the motion of the bus coax her to sleep.

The lurching of the bus into the downtown station shook Kitsune awake. She grabbed her bag and got to her feet as the vehicle came to a stop. She had a list of things to accomplish today before she could get the op going tomorrow. By noon she had accomplished several of them and was sitting in a diner waiting for Betty to meet her.

She had picked a place well in the back where she could watch everyone coming and going. No one except her mom knew she was coming to Saint Louis, but some habits were hard to break. Betty arrived about ten minutes later. She walked through the door, and everyone's attention was immediately drawn to her. She was dressed in a tight black miniskirt and a floral print blouse with the top three buttons open. Kitsune raised her hand and motioned to come to the back of the restaurant.

"I should charge you extra just for making me come in here." Betty gave her a disapproving stare as she slid into the seat.

"Sorry, I am new in town and haven't got the lay of the land yet."

"Yeah, okay, whatever." She glanced at her cell phone and placed it on the table. "Divorced or discharged?"

"I am sorry?"

"Listen, honey. For me, time is literally money. I need to know if you're working to get this guy divorced or discharged."

"Uh, neither."

"Honey, can we put our cards on the table?"

"Sure."

"This isn't my first trip to the circus. You don't look like you can afford to give gifts like me on a regular basis. So, you must have another reason for me to entertain your friend. If you let me know what it is, I can help you get it and let you know how much extra it's going to cost."

"Extra?"

"Yeah, but we'll get to that. Let me know the con you're working, and I promise not to tell." She held up two fingers. "Pro's honor."

Kitsune smiled. "Wow, okay then, I guess things are a little different on the other side of the tracks in this town." She drummed her fingers on the table for a minute. "Okay, nothing nefarious, well, not divorce or discharge. I am running a long con, and I need a whole bunch of basic personal information that someone wouldn't share on their public page. It is just the first step in the game, strictly background, but I need his attention to be directed elsewhere. Also, a wide example of voice samples." Kitsune pulled a slim recorder out of her oversized purse.

"Don't worry about it, honey. I got it covered." Betty pulled at her hair and removed a blonde wig, revealing short, spiky black hair. Embedded in the scalp of the wig were microelectronics.

"Just let me have your memory card, and I will get you everything you need."

"Okay..."

Betty reached out and patted Kitsune's hand. "You seem sharp but in unfamiliar waters. Where are you from, hon?"

"Detroit."

"Well, I am sure your working girls were just that there. Saint Louis has become a tech center and is home to a couple big corporations, so the escort services here are more like freelance intelligence-gathering services. Since you are new here, I will get you everything you need, and it'll only cost you five hundred. Cash."

"Cash?"

"Cash, yeah, it's for me, not my boss, and I don't want it showing up on the tax return if you know what I mean."

Kitsune opened her wallet and looked inside. She put her hand on the table and started drumming her fingers again. Betty looked at her phone and started reading a text. Kitsune pulled out all the bills one by one and laid them on the table. Betty patted her on the hand again, and the money disappeared. She started tugging her wig back on.

"One more thing, I need you to give him this." Kitsune pulled out a micro disc labeled Virtual Companion. "He's a huge fan of the game. You can tell him you were one of the models in the beta test. Actually, the best would be if you did not notice him taking it from you."

"I'll see what I can do, hon. What if he opens it and finds me not on it?"

"I imported your files, so you are."

"Well, aren't you clever? After this is over those will get deleted, right? I mean, it's kind of creepy to think about people hanging with a sim of me." Betty got up and slid her hand up Kitsune's arm. "Especially when the real me is so much better." She blew Kitsune a kiss and walked away.

*

The following two days passed excruciatingly slowly. But then she found herself sitting in Blueberry Hill. She had let a college freshman from the nearby Washington University pick her up and was on a stool in the corner by the dartboards. It gave her an unobstructed view of both the door and the bar. The bar was filled with a mix of college students and upscale professionals who still self-identified as edgy. Some of them even were.

She smiled and winked at her "date," then looked back to make sure Vince was still at the bar. He was making time with a brunette who was stirring a rum and Coke with little enthusiasm.

"Be just my fate; he gets lucky before Betty gets here," Kitsune muttered.

She tossed down the last of her Red Bull and vodka and motioned to her "date" that she was going to the little girl's room. She was about halfway through the crowd when Betty came through the door. She was dressed differently than when she had met Kitsune. She was still beautiful, but her makeup was far more subtle, and she had traded in the skirt for designer jeans and a Saligia Entertainment T-shirt. The escort made no move to call attention to herself, but most of the male eyes on the premises fixed on her. She sauntered to the bar and sat on the other side of the girl with the rum and Coke. She did not even look at Vince once. Kitsune's mouth twisted, but she continued into the bathroom. There was nothing more she could do at this point.

Kitsune returned a few minutes later, and the two were still apart. She came back to her "date," who was holding a shot glass and going on and on about teaching her how to throw darts. She grabbed the shot from his hand and pounded it down, then grabbed the darts from the table and threw all three into the bull-seye.

"I have to go."

The college freshman watched open-mouthed as she walked out of the door.

*

Kitsune woke up the next morning hungover and pissed off. She rolled out of bed and grabbed her tablet. She opened a few programs and closed them down. If she did not have the intelligence she needed, then there was no next step, and she did not have enough money to start over. She clutched the tablet fiercely and pulled her arm back, ready to throw it across the room. Then a knock came on the door. She looked at the far wall, then at the door, and dropped the tablet on her pillow. She grabbed her pistol from the small dresser beside the bed and looked through the peephole. Betty was standing in the hallway. Kitsune uncocked the gun and slid it into the back of her Hello Kitty pajamas. She unlocked the door and opened it.

"You don't have to tell me you weren't successful."

"I wasn't. Then what is this?" She handed Kitsune a manila folder.

Kitsune tried to hide the surprise from her face as she slid the contents into her hand. There was a small SD card and three pages neatly typed.

"I included my impressions of the client as well as the complete audio files of our encounter. You should have everything you need." Betty leaned to Kitsune's left side and whispered, "If you like watching, you should have just told me." She pulled back. "Well, I have to go. Call me if you have any other needs that I can service."

Kitsune watched her walk away, and it was only after Betty turned the corner that her voice came back to her. "Thanks..."

She hesitated in the doorway, chewing on her bottom lip for a moment, then closed her door and went back to flop on the thin mattress of the bed. She plugged the SD card into her headphones and started listening. A moment later, a smile broke out on her face. "Oh, this is good." She grabbed her tablet and began keying notes for tonight's run.

Chapter Four

Vince Davidson had only been asleep for a couple of hours when he was jolted awake. He looked around wildly, trying to figure out what had caused the loud crash that had awoken him. Then he saw the lights coming from his front room where the TV was playing. He hesitated for a long moment but then reached up to trigger the panic button he wore around his neck with his left hand while his right hand slid under his pillow to pull out the Harbinger ten-millimeter pistol he kept under there. He slowly got to his feet, padded to the bedroom doorway, and peered around the corner. He could see down the hallway into the den, and there was a young girl in his easy chair flipping through channels on the remote.

Vince took the pistol in two hands and advanced down the hall. "What are you doing in my house?"

Kitsune looked up at Vince and smiled. "Just watching some TV, Vince. Though I have to say I am a little disappointed. With all the green you're pulling in, I expected at least a full wall plasma, not some dinky seventy-two-inch."

"I'm not home a lot to... Wait a minute, who the fuck are you?"

Kitsune put the remote down on the table next to the recliner and reached for her pistol.

"Hold it, don't move, or I'll shoot."

"No, you won't."

"You don't think so?"

"Vince, you have to know I already took the bullets out of that gun, right."

"Nice try."

Kitsune grabbed her pistol and pointed it at Vince, and he responded by pulling the trigger on his gun, which clicked on an empty chamber. Vince pulled the trigger several more times, but nothing happened. Kitsune gestured with her pistol toward the chair opposite her recliner, and Vince sat down.

"What's this all about? If it's a robbery or kidnapping, you'll never get away with it right now..."

"...because there is a squad of highly trained headhunters coming to save you? Actually, they're not, but I am getting ahead of myself. Let's start at the beginning." Kitsune got to her feet. "Mind if I stand? I talk better when I am moving."

Vince just stared at her.

"First, let me say nice house, and I applaud you for not moving into one of those corporate zones that are all function and no feeling. But it was actually your first mistake. You live in a nice neighborhood, but some of your neighbors are not as security conscious as you. So, I could shimmy up your neighbor's drainpipe to their roof and get right over that electrified fence you put in. Next, you had the dogs, which I am sure some people thought was overkill with the fence, but they were just dogs, and dogs love gravy, even gravy laced with sleeping pills shot over a fence in water balloons. They lapped that shit right up and are now taking a nap."

Kitsune walked around a little bit and turned to scan a couple of titles on the bookshelf. She shook her head slowly from side to side and turned to face Vince again. "Now, the voice print identifier on the front door was an excellent choice, but anyone who spent more than twenty minutes talking to you would have a good enough sample to come with a mix tape that can fool it. Once I was in, I had access to your laptop, which took me a good hour to crack. But finally, your initials, your birthdate, your father's initials, his birthdate, all reversed let me in. Once I had that, pretty much the rest of your life was mine. I took the liberty of printing out some of your bank records, some classified client documents, and a couple of emails you got from sassykitty492 to show that I am telling the truth." Kitsune pointed with her gun at the table next to Vince's chair.

Vince grabbed the stack of documents and sifted through them, his face growing more alarmed as he did. But then, he looked up at Kitsune, and a slow smile spread across his face.

"You seem very happy for a man in your position." The hairs on the back of Kitsune's neck stood up. She started to turn her head but stopped when she felt the barrel of a gun pressed against the back of her head. She dropped her pistol and slowly held up her hands.

"You want to know what your mistake was?"

"Sure." Kitsune slowly turned. Standing behind her was a woman almost six feet in height with white hair tied in a tight ponytail. She was powerfully built but extremely attractive, even just wearing a black hoodie. Kitsune recognized her as Apocrypha, one of Sin Eaters' leading operatives.

"Well, one was just bad luck. I have been spending a lot of nights roaming the streets so I could respond quickly. Two, you rerouted Vince's distress signal to East Saint Louis. Vince was born there and would take a bullet before he went back. So, I knew the general alarm was a trick to get us as far away from here as possible."

"Okay, good to know."

"So, what do you want me to do, Vince, call Corpsec, or do I just pop her twice in the back of the head and drag the body out to the dogs?"

Vince paled momentarily, then recovered. "I think first we need to know why she is here. Did one of the other headhunter organizations put you up to this? I bet it was Gladiatrix, wasn't it?"

"I came here to deliver something to you, Vince." Kitsune started to put her hand in the inside pocket of her jacket. Then, she stopped as Apocrypha pulled back the hammer of her gun. "It's just a hard copy."

"Slowly, do it slowly."

Kitsune pulled out a single piece of folded paper. Vince grabbed it from her hands and began poring over it. Then he leaned back in his chair, a look of confusion spreading across his face.

"You did all that to deliver this?"

"Yeah, how else was I going to get you to take my resume seriously? You did post a job opening for a security expert."

"Okay, now I have to kill her."

"Apocrypha, don't be so mean. Is this so different than when you got recruited?"

"I saved your ass from a half dozen drunken bikers. I did not break into your house."

"You both demonstrated your...what's the word...chops. I like her style." Vince leaned back into his chair and started drumming his fingers on the chair. "Yeah, I think I have a nice little intro adventure for you to show her the ropes on now that you have redeemed yourself. Then we will see what the future will hold for both of you."

Chapter Five

Kitsune looked over at Apocrypha. They had been on the road for several hours, and she had not said a single word. She knew they had just met, but it was getting creepy.

"So, Apocrypha..."

"What?"

"Nothing. Just thought it might be a good idea to get to know each other a little since this is our first mission together. Hell, it's my first mission for Vince, period."

"Why?"

"Because if we're going to be partners, we should try to be friends."

Apocrypha turned to look at her; her expression held neither amusement nor anger, just indifference. "We are not partners and certainly not friends. All you really need to know is you are the tech, and I'm the muscle. We go into the complex. You do your hack. I stand around and look intimidating."

"Yeah, but..." Kitsune started to talk again, but the look on Apocrypha's face changed from indifference to one indicating imminent violence was about to ensue. She remembered hanging out at the bars owned by the mafia, and she had learned to recognize that look and to leave those people alone. She closed her mouth and put her headphones on.

The rest of the trip was made in silence. The car sped along at a steady clip of eighty miles an hour. Apocrypha seemed to be able to navigate it around the other vehicles on the road in some sort of Zen-like trance, where she looked straight ahead but was aware of everything around her. At this rate, they would be at their destination in only a couple of hours. She pulled out her phone and pulled the mission parameters. She was still kind of amazed that she had gotten the job, as most security professionals were ex-cops or former intelligence officers. She had broken into Vince's house to prove her qualifications, but she was not sure which way it was going to go. He could just as easily have had her arrested, though with all she knew now about his operation, that wouldn't have been the smartest move.

The mission seemed to be straightforward enough. They were headed toward a corporate research station that had been shut down a couple of years before because of some sort of accident. They had attempted to get it started again, but the AI refused to let them shut down the security protocols. The first team of standard computer professionals had failed to get in and quit the job outright. The team leader even went so far as to indicate the place was haunted. Kitsune chuckled to herself at that. She had seen some AIs get twitchy, but to believe the place had ghosts was kind of farfetched. But not impossible: after Emergence Day when the magic returned, the dead did not rest as quietly as they used to.

She did not have much experience with things like that, though. Detroit had the odd changeling, like every place. However, there was no real magic community to speak of. It had been hammered hard during the opening phase of the invasion and had never really recovered.

The early days had been the hardest and shaped the person she would become; she learned to climb, forage, and do whatever it took to get the food and other items her family needed to survive. She had thought that was going to be the roughest time in her life. Then, a couple of years later, the relief workers from The Word and other organizations showed up. All those sweet government aid funds also attracted the criminal element, and things got harder. She closed her eyes and held them tight against the memory, turning her head toward the window. She turned up the volume of her headphones and lost herself in the music.

*

Kitsune came awake with a start as the car abruptly stopped. She glanced out of the window and found they were in a gas station. She started to ask how close they were, but Apocrypha had already exited the vehicle; pulling off her headphones, Kitsune followed suit. As she stretched and looked around, it appeared they were on the outskirts of a small town. She stuffed her phone into her jeans and headed to the store to get some much-needed caffeine.

"Hey," Apocrypha called to her.

"What...oomph..." A bag collided with her face which she struggled to hold on to.

"Vince says to put those on before we make it to the facility. He wants you to look like a programming specialist, not a street hacker."

"And if I don't want to?"

"Then Vince says I should leave you."

"And you just do whatever Vince says to do."

"Until you start paying me or give me another reason why I should care about your opinion, yeah."

Kitsune turned around and resumed walking toward the store. She would demand a high bonus for hiding her fashion sense. She reached the store as a guy in a cowboy hat was walking out. He stopped to hold the door open for her. She smiled and was halfway into the store when she felt the cowboy smack her on the ass. She spun around, ready to slap his face, but came up short. The cowboy hat was on the ground, and Apocrypha held the man by the back of his neck.

"Say you're sorry to the nice lady."

"Fu—" The rest of the cowboy's sentence was cut off as Apocrypha increased the strength of her grip.

"Say you're sorry."

"I'm sorry."

"Good, now get lost." Apocrypha shoved him toward the parking lot. He glared but said nothing as he found his truck and drove away.

"I could have handled him." Kitsune stuck a finger in Apocrypha's face.

"I repeat, programming expert, not street hacker." Without waiting for a response, Apocrypha started walking back to the car.

Kitsune re-entered the store and asked the clerk where the bathrooms were. He pointed toward the back with a slimy smile on his face.

She spilled the clothes out on the baby changing table. The outfit was so not hers: a simple black skirt, white shirt, and a pair of glasses because everyone knew that for a girl to be smart, she had to wear glasses. She looked over the outfit and thought yep, computer programmer or maybe a Japanese schoolgirl. She wondered which look Vince was going for. The emails from sassykitty492 made her think of a Japanese schoolgirl, and that made her a little queasy. She made a mental note to change back into her regular clothes before they got back to the office.

She started to unbutton her blouse, then thought about the smile on the clerk's face. She pulled a small device out of her purse. She hit the switch, sending out a small wave of magnetic energy that would disrupt most nearby surveillance equipment. Satisfied she had at least a little privacy, she quickly changed her clothes. Once that was done, she exited the bathroom. She headed for the cashier but stopped to grab a couple of bottles of Seizure. The highly caffeinated beverage was something street hackers and programming experts had in common.

The clerk had his back to her and was beating on a small monitor, trying to get it to show something other than snow.

"Can I pay for these?'

The clerk turned around. "That will be four ninety-six. Hey, you aren't going up to the Synapse research facility, are you?"

"Why would you think that?"

"Cuz you're driving a new car. The only people around here who drive new cars are going there. I wouldn't do it if I were you. Selene has gotten violent."

"Selene?"

"Yeah, Selene, wow, your boss didn't tell you anything." He leaned closer over the counter. "Selene Logain and her husband were hot-shot scientists at Synapse. They say he died in the fire. They never recovered the body, and she refused to leave when they closed the facility. She said she would not go home without him and eventually died up there of a broken heart. Her ghost still walks the hall trying to find him."

"Okay, thanks for the heads-up." She shoved a five his way and scooped up the bottles.

"The other guys did not believe either, but when they tried to reopen the center, it didn't go well for them. That was when the deaths started happening."

"I knew I recognized you. You were on that *Scooby-Doo* episode."

"What's *Scooby-Doo*?"

Kitsune found that question the spookiest thing he had said and quickly went out of the door and headed for the car. Apocrypha was already in the driver's seat and tapping her fingers on the steering wheel. As soon as Kitsune closed the door, they were off.

"So, what do you think about this whole ghost business?" Kitsune handed Apocrypha a bottle of Seizure, which, surprisingly, she took.

"Don't believe in them; it's probably another corp trying to get access to the facility using some plot they stole from *Scooby-Doo*."

"You watch *Scooby-Doo*, me too."

"I watched *Scooby-Doo* when I was six." Apocrypha turned her face back to the road and ignored Kitsune's attempts at further conversation until they reached the facility. She pulled the car into a parking space. The lot was empty except for one other vehicle, a sedan with a huge man, whose job title was probably chauffeur but who was more like a bodyguard, standing by the passenger door. Apocrypha got out of the car and opened the trunk. It was full of gear and weapons, but she just pulled out a large handgun, which she put into a shoulder harness. Kitsune grabbed her backpack with her computer tech and looked around for her gun.

"Hey, where's mine?"

"It's back at the office. I thought we went over this. You're brains, I'm brawn."

"If you think I am going on a mission with people or things out to stop us without having protection, you're nuts."

Apocrypha got an exasperated look on her face but, after a moment, reached into the trunk and pulled out a small pistol, which she handed to Kitsune.

"Thank you." Kitsune looked at her outfit and shoved the pistol into her purse. *Vince is not going to get to pick my wardrobe for the next mission.*

They heard the sedan's door open, and a balding man in an expensive suit got out. Apocrypha stepped slightly in front of Kitsune so the corp would not see her putting the gun in her purse.

"Mr. Bangura, I was not aware that you were going to meet us here personally." Apocrypha walked across the parking lot and offered her hand to the executive. He took it, but he made no attempt to hide that he thought shaking hands with the "hired help" was beneath him.

"Vincent said you two were his best, most experienced operatives and could handle this quickly and without fanfare. I hoped he was not lying as much as usual."

"We will take care of your problem. Have no doubts."

"That was what the last group said. This facility was once our most treasured research station. Then, due to an operator error, the AI turned on us and locked us out of the station. It shut itself off from all outside access. We are restarting the research but have discovered there was some information on this location's mainframe that we have not been able to duplicate. I need you to get into the facility, restart the system, get all the files marked project outreach, then purge the AI. Can you do that?"

"Miss Fox is more than capable of doing all that, and I will ensure that no one interferes with her."

Mr. Bangura did not seem particularly impressed but returned to his car without responding to Apocrypha. Kitsune shared a glance with Apocrypha and started walking toward the front door. The building was large and looked out of place in this rustic setting with its obvious security features. The door was sealed and had no obvious way in except for a tiny keypad on the side.

"It's funny; this setup is so old that it's probably effective again. Nowadays, everything is a voice print matcher or at least a retina scanner. Luckily, I have a fondness for old tech." She reached over and punched a ten-digit code, opening the door.

Apocrypha raised an eyebrow. "How did you do that?"

"Way back when these were popular, some people stopped paying for their security services and hid in the buildings to avoid them coming to collect on the bill. The companies then implemented a ten-digit code known only to their employees that opened any of the locks."

"And you know this how?"

Kitsune knew because when she lived in Detroit, she had spent two days starving, entering every combination she could think of to access a food store's warehouse. She stumbled on the right number by pure luck, but that was not a story she would share with Apocrypha. "I slept with the manager of the company."

Apocrypha nodded like that was the answer she had expected and pulled out a pair of shades. The glasses shifted tint from yellow to red, and she peeked inside. The building was dark, but with the light coming from behind, they could see soot and fire damage to the walls. The reports indicated there had been a blaze on the night they shut down the facility, but no other details about the incident had been given. She looked down the hall, and the infrared sensors in the glasses sprung to life, indicating that she and Kitsune were the only ones in the immediate area.

"Let's go."

Their heels echoed down the passageways as they walked to the central processing unit. After a few moments, they arrived at another door with a keypad, which Kitsune opened in short order. The door opened into a small room filled with windows, allowing viewing into the next room. That was obviously some sort of medical facility with shelves filled with drugs, a group of examining tables, and, in the corner, a giant safe. The door connecting the two rooms had no handles or even a keypad, just a small knob with an antenna. Apocrypha gestured toward the door.

"Now what?"

"The door is controlled by the mainframe. We have to get it running again to access the room, and then I have to get into that safe, which might take a while. It looks like a serious piece of work."

The duo turned around to try to find their way to the mainframe room. They stopped dead in their tracks as they were confronted by a shadowy apparition of a middle-aged woman.

"Get out!" the ghost shrieked at them.

"Fuck!" Kitsune dropped to the floor.

Apocrypha pulled her pistol and shot in one smooth motion. The bullets slid through the ghost, dissipating its form, and impacting the wall behind it. Apocrypha grabbed Kitsune by the shirt collar and pulled her to her feet and out of the door. As they raced into the hallway, the shadow reformed. The ghost's cry echoed down the corridor, but it was not a vengeful sound; it was more like a heart breaking in sorrow.

Kitsune and Apocrypha stopped running when they reached the cafeteria.

"Okay, this place might be haunted," Apocrypha said as she put a fresh clip into her gun.

"You think?"

"Maybe. Then again, it could just be a hologram."

"I have seen a lot of entertainment in my time, and no machine could have made that sound."

"Maybe, but we still have a job to do."

"You know, you have quite the work ethic."

"It happens when it's all you have." Apocrypha slid the pistol back into her holster. "But it didn't seem to be able to affect us, so let's find the mainframe and get paid."

"Not affect us, I think it affected us."

"Making you pee your pants is not enough of an effect to make us stop. Let's go." Apocrypha stepped out into the hallway and looked both ways. The passageway was empty, and she started walking.

They traveled down the corridor with their senses alert for any further visitation by the ghost, but none appeared. Soon, they found themselves in front of the entrance to the mainframe area. The first area was easily accessed and led to a room full of terminals, but there was a secondary area visible through a small glass panel in the door, which had a more sophisticated setup and a body hunched over the desk.

"Okay, I should be able to use one of these terminals to hack into the system and open that door. Once we get in there, we should have control over the whole facility." Kitsune spoke matter-of-factly but kept peering toward the body in the other room.

"What is it?" Apocrypha finally said.

"You don't think that's, you know..."

"A *what*?"

"Zombie."

"There are no such things as zombies." Kitsune frowned at Apocrypha. "Okay, there are such things as zombies, but there aren't any around here."

"Yeah, because we haven't run into anything supernatural around here."

"Listen, you want to hang out here overnight or get the job done and leave while the sun is still in the sky?"

"You have a point." Kitsune sat down, pulled out her gear, and started to type furiously on the keyboard. Apocrypha stood over her, watching intently for several minutes until Kitsune turned around.

"You know how hard it is to type with someone looking over your shoulder. Go patrol or something."

"And what if the ghost comes back?"

"Trust me, you'll know right away."

*

It took Kitsune the better part of an hour, but she was able to overcome the first level of security on the terminals. She then pulled out her interface plugs and dove into the virtual world.

She remembered how much her first visit to the virtual world had changed her life. As her connection with the family deepened, the money started to get surprisingly good.

An intelligent person would have put the money away for a rainy day. However, she had learned a lesson during those first days of the conflict that sometimes Zeus skipped the rain and went straight for the lightning bolt that fried your ass regardless of how much money you had. So, when she got money, she spent it. Usually, this resulted in an incredibly fun evening that she could barely remember, but one time, she took a trip to New York and found herself in a high-end café trading drinks with the so-called computer elite. Mostly, they seemed like overstuffed Eurotrash. There had been one who seemed a little interesting. He had invited her back to his office to check out the latest in computer technology. She wasn't interested in him or the tech but thought the mob might be, so she figured she could check out the security and come back for a run later in the month. Soon, she found herself in the center of the R+D section. He asked if she had ever jacked into the web. He was also putting his hands all over her, so she figured she would cut it short when he slid an induction helmet onto her head. Suddenly, her vision exploded with a thousand colors she had never seen before, and she hurtled down the rabbit hole. She was part of the net, and it was part of her. As she concentrated on different tasks, the software instantly complied. A giant grin spread over her face; she had been looking for a new world without knowing it, and here it was. She was completely engrossed for an hour, then the connection faded as the tech removed the helmet. He was sitting looking at her expectantly. The next morning, he woke after the best night of his life to a completely empty room.

Once she started to know what she was doing, she got herself a couple of interface plugs so she could connect her brain directly to the web. The equipment allowed her to access the system and her intrusion programs like they were a physical reality. She flicked the switch and was suddenly in a black ninja outfit with pockets filled with lock picks and other things to circumvent security. Her preferred environment for runs was a medieval Japanese city, but the AI had overruled her protocols, and she was in a burning building. She had encountered this situation before in highly secure facilities, but this seemed different, as if it were replicating the last night of the location's operation.

She walked down the halls of the lab while people rushed past her as the flames climbed up the side of the walls. They did not seem to notice her, so she assumed they were only graphics and not an actual part of the program. She retraced the steps she had just taken in the real world and entered the room containing the mainframe. As she walked in, she found Mr. Bangura arguing with another man.

"Mr. Logain, we have to hurry and get copies of all the research before the fire takes the whole building down."

"I don't understand how this could have happened. The fire suppression system should have kicked in, and our link to the corporate network should still be active even in case of disasters." Mr. Logain turned his back to Bangura and began to type commands into the computer.

"Maybe we were victims of corporate espionage."

"Yeah, but the only people who had commands for all those systems are me and you." Mr. Logain whirled around. "Did you do this? That makes no sense. There are going to be hundreds of deaths, and the research has been unsuccessful. It's worthless."

"Not to me." Mr. Bangura pulled a gun from his coat pocket. "Now open the access to the mainframe."

"Okay, just don't shoot." Mr. Logain typed furiously, and a moment later, there was a click as the door to the mainframe opened.

"Thank you. Now your services are no longer required." The pistol went off, and Mr. Logain's head snapped back as the bullet went through his skull. His body collapsed onto the table and lay still.

Kitsune ran to the table, momentarily forgetting that all of this was not real. Her hands passed through Mr. Logain.

Mr. Bangura stood for a moment, a slow smile spreading

across his face. He took a step, then stopped at the sound of support beams cracking over his head. Before he could react, a portion of the roof collapsed down, pinning him to the floor. Mr. Logain took the opportunity to stumble into the mainframe room and close the door behind him.

Mr. Bangura pushed at the flaming debris, unable to get any leverage to shift it off him.

Kitsune smiled, thinking he was dead, but then she realized that all this had happened years ago. She knew he lived.

"Brian!" A woman rushed into the room. Kitsune recognized the voice as that of the ghost.

"Over here, help me out," Mr. Bangura called out to Selene. Selene immediately rushed to his side and pulled his body free of the debris.

"Where's Brian?"

"I'm not sure."

Selene skirted the flaming pockets of the room and looked into the mainframe room. "He's just hunched over the terminal and not moving. We have to get in there."

Mr. Bangura grabbed her by the shoulders. "He was the only one with the access codes; he must have been overcome by smoke while trying to restart the emergency response systems."

"Nooo!" Selene started to bang on the door over and over.

"We have to go. He would not have wanted you to perish too." Mr. Bangura dragged Selene away as she wept and screamed.

"Wow, what an incredible bastard!" Kitsune watched as the two left. She'd known she would probably be working for corporate pricks, but this was more than she had bargained for. The flames grew higher, then the whole room faded to black nothingness with just a floating prompt.

Kitsune walked up and spoke. "Selene." The blackness shifted into a series of menus, allowing her access to the mainframe. On her left was a series of windows corresponding to the security monitors, which were apparently still online. One view was of the cafeteria, where she could see Apocrypha walking around.

*

Apocrypha walked out of the door and glanced in both directions down the hall. There was nothing to be seen, and she started to make her way back to the cafeteria, wondering what the shelf life of a Twinkie was. As she entered the room and approached the vending machines, she noticed a flicker of movement out of the corner of her eye. As she turned to see what had caught her attention, a chair slid across the floor toward her. She stopped it with her foot and looked around. There was nothing to be seen, and she appeared to be alone in the room. Then, the drawers across the room opened by themselves, and the silverware floated in the air for a moment before launching itself at her. She threw herself down and knocked a table over, creating a barrier between her and the knives that hurtled toward her. The knives struck with such force that they pieced through the table but did not reach her. She reached her hand to the side of the table to give her the leverage to get up. Before she could move, a table from across the room flipped over and slammed into her. She let loose a scream as she was sandwiched between the two tables, and the knives impaled her in a dozen places. Her hand quivered for a moment, then lay still.

Chapter Six

Kitsune heard the scream both through her virtual connection and her actual ears. She surged to her feet, the interface plugs coming unplugged as she stood, interrupting her connection to the mainframe. She ran for the hallway, but as she reached the door, a body blocked her path, knocking her backward. The chauffeur's large frame filled the doorway. She stepped back, and the chauffeur's hand shot out and grabbed her around the neck. She instinctively reached for her pistol but remembered it was in her purse on the table. The chauffeur held her, pinning her arms to her side. He lifted her off the floor and pressed her to the wall.

Mr. Bangura strode languidly into the room and watched Kitsune flail about. "You're as good as your boss promised. I am impressed. Now, I just need you to grant me access to the mainframe, and your services will no longer be required."

"Just like Mr. Logain," Kitsune gasped.

"How did you know that? Well, it matters not. You will do what

I want, or your life will be short and painful. I need that research."

Kitsune struggled against the chauffeur to no avail, but she thought she could see someone over the chauffeur's shoulders.

"Hey, asshole, anything you have to say to my coworker, you need to say to me first."

Kitsune fell to the floor as the chauffeur released his grip and turned to face Apocrypha. She was covered in still-bleeding wounds and seemed barely able to stand. The chauffeur said nothing but rushed at Apocrypha. Kitsune did not want to watch. She knew that Apocrypha would normally take this guy apart, but in her current condition, she had no chance.

Apocrypha stood her ground and, at the last possible moment, spun under the chauffeur's outstretched arms and planted one of the knives from the kitchen into the soft tissue at the base of his neck. He stiffened and pitched to the floor.

Apocrypha took a moment, then, with a visible effort, stood straight up. She pulled her pistol and aimed it at Mr. Bangura.

"Article Seventeen of the contract indicates that any hostile act toward a headhunter operative voids the contract, relinquishes all funds, and allows the operative to take whatever action they feel is necessary to safeguard themselves." The gun boomed three times.

As the bullets sped toward Mr. Bangura, they slowed and stopped. Mr. Bangura's eyes focused in concentration, and the bullets reversed trajectory and impacted Apocrypha, knocking her off her feet.

Mr. Bangura then turned to Kitsune and gestured toward her. She rose off the floor and looked directly at him.

"So, I guess the research wasn't a failure."

"No, we discovered a way to enhance certain parts of the brain so that psychic potential was unleashed. I decided that I was the only one who would have this power."

"So, you started the fire and severed the network links, but Brian stopped you from getting to the research files."

"Yes, something that you will now remedy."

Kitsune could see a black mist congealing behind Mr. Bangura.

"I can't believe that Selene rescued the man who killed her husband."

"Yes, that stupid cow actually thought I was trying to save him. Now you are going to open that door, or what I did to your friend is going to look like mercy."

"Okay, but one question: what are you going to do about the ghost?"

"I don't believe in ghosts."

"Ah, but I think they believe in you." Kitsune managed to indicate with a nod, and Mr. Bangura turned to look behind him.

The black mist had coalesced into the shape of a young woman. After a moment, it fractured into a face that looked like it had spent years slowly rotting away. Mr. Bangura dropped Kitsune and directed his power to the objects in the room. He sent everything he could at Selene, but it all passed harmlessly through her form. However, when she reached out to him, her hands were solid enough to wrap around his throat, and he screamed. Selene increased her pressure, and his screams were silenced. A moment later, there was a nauseating thud as his neck snapped.

Selene dropped Mr. Bangura and drifted toward Kitsune. She mouthed the words "thank you" and was gone.

Kitsune crawled over and pulled Apocrypha into her lap, wrapping one arm around her. She pulled out her phone and dialed 9-1-1 with one hand. "Hold on, partner. This is just going to be the first of our adventures. You're not allowed to quit on me."

Chapter Seven

Apocrypha awoke to someone grabbing her arm and sticking her with a pointed object. She reacted instinctively and grabbed the outstretched arm. Pain shot through her body.

"Ow, let go of me. I'm your nurse. I'm your nurse."

Apocrypha opened her eyes, taking in the white walls and room full of monitoring equipment. She let go of the nurse's arm.

"Sorry."

"It's okay. We did not think you were going to be conscious for days with your injuries. Are you a changeling?"

"Yeah. Yeah. I'm something like that."

"Well, the doctors are going to need some more information to assist in treating you."

"No, no, they are not. Just treat me like everybody else and be happy when I leave a couple days early." Apocrypha looked around and saw her cell phone sitting on the table. She grabbed it and flipped it open. The nurse was standing with the needle, watching her. "You can go, help somebody else."

"I was going to give you something to ease your pain and help you rest."

"Don't need anything like that. Me and pain are longtime good friends."

She watched the nurse leave her room, then brought up her messages, one from the new chick, six from Vince, and a text from her dad's doctor with a number for a street shaman named Sanders. Her finger danced around the keyboard as she tried to decide who to call first. Before she could hit a number, her phone started ringing. The caller ID popped up: Vince. The thought that he had paid the nurse to call him the moment she woke up was not a good sign. She clenched her other hand into a fist and answered the phone.

"Vince, calling to check on your valued employee. How touching."

"Uh, Yeah, sure. Listen, I got a priority one, and I need you."

"Are you fucking kidding me? You realize you are calling me while I am still in the hospital. I am in here because, wait for it, you sent me on a supposed low-tier mission and forbade me from carrying any of my usual arms or protection. You thought it would look bad for the client if I showed up looking like, you know, a headhunter. Not to mention, I was persona non grata to you a couple of days ago."

"Yeah, that was a bad call. It turns out that the guy was working on his own and not on behalf of the client. I found that out when I tried to bill them. And you know if I don't get paid, I might have to pull back your paycheck cuz..."

"Vince, I have confidence that you found a way to get paid and will find a way to pay me and Kit-su-what's-her-name for the high-tier job that this should have been categorized as or, come tomorrow, I am Battle Brothers' employee."

"You hate those guys. Besides, there was like one ghost."

"I do hate them, but they pay people on time, and you're forgetting about the telekinetic psychotic client."

"Okay. Fine. All right, now for tonight's mission."

"Vince, I am in the hospital. I am not going on a mission."

"It's a head-up job; I got nobody else. It's a tier three, but I'll pay as tier four."

"Which probably means it's a tier five. No, actually, fuck no. Goodbye." She clicked the disconnect button, then entered the shaman's number.

"Sanders."

"Hey, this is Apocrypha. I think you might be expecting my call."

"Oh yeah, I got the gist from your dad's doctor. Pretty nasty stuff, it's going to cost you, but I can help."

"How much?"

Sanders told her. It wasn't good news.

"Okay, I will have the first part to you on Friday and the rest after he gets better."

"The rest after the ceremony, twisted stuff like in your dad. I make no promises."

"Fine, after the ceremony."

Apocrypha made a mental tally of her bank balance and clicked redial under Vince's number.

*

Apocrypha slammed the door of the cab with her foot as she struggled with the lid of the pain meds; the only thing she had agreed to when she signed herself out of the hospital. She choked a handful down as she walked up the steps and looked up at the scanner above the door. After a moment, she heard the lock click, and she entered. She tried to walk normally; however, each step sent an echo of agony up her body. She stopped, took a deep breath, then forced herself to continue as if the pain did not exist. She knew better than to show weakness around here. She walked quickly to the op center and skidded to a stop as she found Kitsune and M'rey standing around the planning table.

"What are you doing here?"

M'rey looked up nervously. He was dressed in a blue suit and an orange tie. He was twirling an engraved wand in his hand and stopped when he looked at Apocrypha. "Vince told me to scout out the location and check to see if they had any mystic protections."

"Not you, her."

Kitsune put the papers in her hand down. "Her? Her has a name, Kitsune. You know; the girl who saved your ass."

"You called the meat wagon. That doesn't count as saving my ass. Now, answer the question."

"I'm going on an op to recover a kidnapped employee. Why are you here?"

"First off, he was not kidnapped. It was a hostile acquisition; under the corporate legal code, they are completely different, and this op is mine."

"No way, Vince said this one is mine. Besides, I need the cash. And you should still be in the hospital."

"I heal quick. What do you need the cash for?"

"Rent, I'm kind of broke. Not that it's any of your business since we aren't partners."

"You're broke. We just got paid yesterday. How did you go through fifteen hundred in one night?"

Kitsune chewed on her lip and looked around for a moment. "Stuff."

"Hey, you're right; it's none of my business. But you're not ready for a full run against dedicated opposition."

"Not even if I have the keys to their security system?"

Apocrypha hesitated a long moment. "Fine, you can run overwatch, but you're not going in."

Kitsune opened her mouth but then just nodded.

"Okay, now show me the plans for the building and what you found."

*

Apocrypha stood in the shadows of the door, watching as the guard walked by, then eased out of the darkness.

"Hey there, got a light?"

The guard was quick and professional; he was already pulling his pistol from its holster when Apocrypha hit him with the taser. The gun was thrown from his grasp as he fell to the ground, and she hit him a couple more times with the taser until he was unconscious.

"Shouldn't you have done some sort of super karate move and knocked him out soundlessly?" Kitsune's voice came through Apocrypha's earpiece.

"Not on the menu tonight." Apocrypha slipped over to the door and looked around. "Are you in yet?"

"You know, people hate it when you ask that question. There was this guy I used to see. He was the accountant for the Don, and when I had to ask that question, he would take it very personally."

"Kit-sun-ee, are you in yet?"

"Almost there. This is not as easy as you think it is. I mean, if you want to, we can switch positions. I can go in the side door while you hang outside the windows on the twenty-eighth floor."

"You volunteered for that, not that I understand why you're

there. Most hackers I know sit in a room thirty miles away and just click a mouse."

"Would not have worked. Thanatos has all the security protocols on a closed network with no outside access. The good news for us is that the executives on the upper floors still want their Wi-Fi connectivity. So, if you get close enough to the windows, it's like you're in the office. Plus, I can look at people's desks and see who has their password stuck on their desk with sticky notes. This makes the hack the easy part of the night. There!"

There was a loud click as the door in front of Apocrypha unlocked.

Apocrypha opened the door slightly, looked around, then slid in. According to Vince's sources, the company relied mostly on its high-tech security system and a few guards to patrol the outside and keep troublemakers away.

"Okay, your target is on the tenth floor of the executive apartments. I will send an elevator to you and close down the others."

"'kay."

"Hey, partner."

"We're not partners."

"Just checking."

Apocrypha reached up and took off her headset, which let Kitsune communicate with her. She gripped it very tightly for a moment, then put it back on.

"Here, I got something for you," Kitsune's voice chimed in. A small map popped on a HUD on Apocrypha's glasses, showing the route to the service elevators. The route was short, and Apocrypha was soon on her way up.

The elevator opened on the tenth floor, and Apocrypha walked out. The decor was expensive and nice, in the bland, don't offend anyone style that characterized most corporate living arrangements.

"Not bad for a prison," Apocrypha said to no one in particular.

"You talking to me?"

"Nope," Apocrypha said under her breath. In a louder voice, she added, "Can you give me the picture of that guy again?"

The display of the map faded and was replaced with a picture of a clean-cut young executive type. His corporate name tag read Corey Givens.

"So, you said this wasn't a kidnapping."

"Not when a major company does it. The latest form of corporate recruitment is to send in a black ops team to pick up your competition's greatest intellects from their home and spirit them off to a new research center where they will work for you or face certain death. When that happens, the aggrieved parties call people like us to get them back. Some groups are even given orders that if they can't retrieve the talent, they should eliminate them. Vince doesn't offer that, or at least he's smart enough not to try sending me on one."

"Okay, but I still don't get why it's not kidnapping."

"Because it's a standard operating procedure at this point, and nobody goes to the cops, and nobody goes to war over it. It's just the price of doing business in the twenty-first century."

Apocrypha came to a central hub with four spokes leading to apartments and a glass viewing area at each end. The hub was complete with a statue of a metallic abstract piece that, as far as Apocrypha could tell, meant absolutely nothing.

She turned down the corridor to the east and found the apartment, which had been identified as where Mr. Givens was staying. In contrast to the high-tech trappings, it had a very conventional key lock. Apocrypha bent down on one knee to work on the lock.

"You want me to run down there and take care of that."

"No, I can handle it."

"You sure? It would be no trouble. I could be right there. Holy crap, you got incoming."

The brass work of the door was highly shined, and Apocrypha caught the side of a blur coming toward her head at almost the exact moment Kitsune called out the alarm. She reacted by instinct and rolled backward as a huge mass of flesh impacted the ground where she was. She came back onto her hands and did a handstand, driving her heels into the creature that had tried to squash her. The creature rocked backward, and she used her momentum to spring to her feet. The impact sent a stabbing pain through her side, and she knew she must have torn her stitches out. She clenched her teeth against the pain and whirled around, drawing her pistol and sighting down in one motion, then she stopped dead.

The creature was the size of an ogre or half-giant but was formed entirely differently. Apocrypha's mind raced back to when she was growing up and read an account of an American soldier who had been at one of the Nazi concentration camps. He had described finding the bodies piled in the cold, which had frozen together so that you never knew where one person started and the next ended. That image had haunted her for a long time. Now she was confronted with it again, except the bodies were still moving this time.

"What the hell is that?" Kitsune screamed in her earpiece. This broke Apocrypha from her shock, and she fired the gun. The shots rang out, tearing pieces of flesh and sending blood spewing. The creature itself seemed to take no notice. However, the bodies that comprised it screamed in agony. The beast lumbered forward, and Apocrypha turned and ran.

"You got a plan?"

"Running seems to be working for the moment." The creature pursued Apocrypha, but it was malformed and, while possessed of great strength, slow. Apocrypha looked wildly about as she quickly approached the end of the hallway. All that waited for her was a large window that took up the whole wall and a long drop. Apocrypha got an idea.

"Is there a janitorial closet on this level?"

"You know, I understand if you had an accident in this situation, and I might have one too. Are you sure now is the time to clean up?"

"Kitsune!"

"The closet is down the hall to your left. It's an electronic lock. Give me a second."

Apocrypha saw the door pop open and sprinted toward it. Once inside, she sorted through the materials and pulled out a large keg of cleaning formula. Apocrypha turned to leave with her prize and found the creature had barred her way. She grabbed a vial from her belt and threw it into the creature's face. The creature screamed and clawed its face to get the liquid off. Apocrypha took the opening, tossed the keg through its legs, and followed the cleaner face first.

Apocrypha hit the other side of the hallway hard.

"Acid?" Kitsune questioned.

"Holy water, no way that thing is natural."

Apocrypha's foot shot out and kicked the cleaner down the hallway. She was still struggling to regain her feet when the creature got its hands on her and threw her headlong down the hallway. Apocrypha went limp to try to roll with the impact, but it did little to soften the blow. She hit hard, and she swore a rib snapped. She felt herself on the verge of losing consciousness. She closed and opened her eyes, focusing on the here and now, marshaling her will so as not to collapse. She rose and loaded a new clip into her forty-five. Without looking, she kicked the cleaner the rest of the distance to the window with the back of her ankle. The creature was closing the space between them, and she threw her remaining vial of holy water at its head. It roared in fury and surged forward.

Apocrypha turned and unloaded her pistol, using her first shots to explode the cleaning fluid and the rest to shatter the window. She took a three-step setup and leaped, grabbing the top of the shattered window. The glass cut into her hand, one more source of agony to add to the pile, but she held on and swung her legs up into the air ten stories up as the creature slid on the cleaner and flew out of the building to fall to the ground below. Apocrypha swung back into the building and landed on the floor. She took one step, lost her footing on the cleaner, and almost followed the creature out of the window. She grabbed the drapes and pulled herself to safety.

"Hey, Apocrypha... Are you still with me, partner?"

Apocrypha started to correct Kitsune but did not have the strength. "I'm here."

"I thought that might have been you who went out the window."

"Nope, that was the other guy."

Apocrypha got up, returned to the target's apartment, and kicked the door in. There seemed no sense in being quiet now. The scientist cowered on the floor, holding a pistol in his shaking grip.

"I guess he had heard the stories of the elimination teams, too," Kitsune observed. "You going to be nice?"

"I am all out of nice."

Apocrypha took three steps forward, grabbed the gun out of

his hand, and shoved hers in his face.

"Who the fuck are you, *and what the fuck was that*?"

"I'm nobody, and I don't know." The scientist slunk back-ward, trying to get the gun out of his face.

"Listen, I am on a mission to retrieve you for your old corp, but unless I get some more information, I am inclined to let you make your own way back."

"I work in next-gen development, trying to retrofit alien tech to be mass-produced. About a month ago, I presented a pa-per about creating a cybernetic interface that magical beings could use. The next thing I know, I get grabbed off the street. I figured, what the hell? This is just part of corporate employment, but when they told me I was going to work at an office in northern Illinois, I started to try and find a way out. That monstrosity showed up the next day. All I know about it is that it scared the hell out of me."

"Fucking peachy." Apocrypha understood why a northern Il-linois location had scared Givens. That meant Chicago, which meant criminals and dark magic. What had Vince got her involved with now? She was set to question him further when her headset buzzed. "*What?*"

"So, I have bad news and worse news."

"Well, that's a change of pace; let's start with the bad news."

"That maneuver set off every alarm I had deactivated."

"So, what's the worse news?"

"That thing you threw out of the building is getting up. It left a couple of bodies on the ground, but it's standing up and looks to be getting ready for round two."

Apocrypha closed her eyes for a long second. "All right, call M'rey. I am going to need a magical extraction." She put her gun back in its holster and reached her hand out.

"Are you going to kill me?" Givens did not seem reassured by the gesture.

"No!" Apocrypha made a real effort to calm herself; none of this was the scientist's fault. "I am just going to take you back to your old life. Take my hand, and we can get out of here."

The scientist came to his feet, a resigned look on his face, like he still wasn't sure but did not have any better options.

Apocrypha pulled the scientist close to her with one hand and put her other hand out to the wall to steady herself.

"Kitsune, is he ready?"

"M'rey is online, but he says he can't get a read on you."

"Yeah." Apocrypha reached up and pulled down her hood, whispering very softly, "Nachte finis." There was a brief swirl of light as the magic of her garment, which protected her from magical scrying, shut down.

"Now's he got you."

"And I wonder who else does." Apocrypha felt the floor under her shift, then the room around her faded from view. The next moment, she found herself on the floor of M'rey's study, puking her guts. She did not like teleporting even when the mage had time to be gentle about the landing, and this had not been one of those occasions. After the contents of her stomach were emptied, she rolled over on her back.

"I am getting way too old for this shit." She looked up at M'rey, then over at Givens, who was still puking. She closed her eyes, too spent to worry about getting him taken care of. What little strength had been carrying her was gone, and she faded into exhaustion.

Chapter Eight

Apocrypha awoke to a gentle prodding and slowly opened her eyes. She glanced to the side of her bed, and her eyes opened much wider. Her teddy bear had apparently jumped off the shelf where it had sat for several years and climbed onto the bed and was poking her in an attempt to get her up. Apocrypha rolled over and pulled her pistol from under her pillow.

"Hi, Mr. Bear. So, let's see which one of two things is going on at the moment. One, I had a psychotic break from all the stress I have been under lately, or two, a certain mage practitioner is having fun at my expense, not knowing that I own several large caliber weapons and know where his computer is that contains almost a terabyte of music and porn. You have to wonder does he feel lucky."

"Wow, you have no sense of humor in the morning. I am glad I had Mr. Bear wake you up. You would have probably shot me."

"That would have been a distinct possibility." Apocrypha sat up and pulled the blankets up to keep her body covered. She looked down at herself and over at the dresser with her clothes hanging on them.

M'rey held up his hands. "It wasn't me. Vince had the meat wagon come in and stitch you up again, and then Kitsune put you to bed."

"How long...?"

"Two days. Vince said it would be best to leave you alone, but he kind of ran out of patience and made me come up to check if you were still alive."

"I think so." Apocrypha reached down and ran a hand over the new scars that had been added to her body. "You got anything to eat?"

"Nope, but Kitsune left you some stuff on your dresser." Apocrypha looked over to find beer and pizza on her nightstand. She hesitated for a moment, then got up and grabbed some of the food. The pizza was cold, and the beer was warm, but she choked a slice down. "Thanks for the exit strategy last night."

"No problem. You know, when I establish a connection to do a remote teleport, I get glimpses into people, right?"

"Yeah."

"So, was it something that manifested on Emergence Day?"

Apocrypha took a deep breath. "No, my bloodline is a little older than that. Listen, now is not the best time to discuss this. Let me get dressed and talk to Vince. I'll come to find you later. Do me a favor, and don't talk to anybody before that."

"Um, sure, I mean everybody's got secrets, right."

M'rey got up and walked toward the door, then turned around and raised an eyebrow. Mr. Bear jumped off the bed and climbed back onto the shelf where he usually sat. Apocrypha looked at M'rey with a troubled look on her face as he opened the door.

"Hey, did Vince want anything else?" she said as he was on his way out.

"Well..."

"He has a new assignment for me, doesn't he?"

"Yeah."

"I should have known. Okay, I will get dressed and head down to his office; that will teach me to pass out at work."

"It does make it easy for the boss to find you."

"Is Givens okay?"

"Yeah, he was spooked, but they cleaned him up and put him someplace safe until his company can come get him."

Apocrypha got up and started grabbing clothes at random, putting them on while trying to consume another piece of pizza. She opened a can, took a swig of the beer, and spit it out into the waste basket. Cold pizza was one thing. Warm beer was another entirely.

She finished getting dressed and headed to the back steps that led to the gym. She was halfway down the steps when she ran into Kitsune coming up.

"Oh, hey, you're awake."

"Yeah, guess I was out of it for a little while. What are you doing here?"

"I work here."

"Yeah, I know, that's not..."

"Vince has me plugging all the holes I poked in his security systems. I guess I should get back to that." Kitsune slid past Apocrypha. Apocrypha took a couple more steps down and turned.

"Kitsune."

"Yeah, what?" Kitsune had an annoyed look on her face.

"Thanks for the pizza."

"You're welcome."

Apocrypha smiled weakly and continued down the steps and around the corner to the door of the workout area. She slowly opened the door and peeked inside. When she saw it was empty, she walked in. She made her way to the center mat, then bent over and touched her toes before stretching to the left and the right. She healed quickly but needed to know what was still injured before she talked to Vince about any other jobs. She was desperate but not stupid.

"All right, let's see what we still got." She launched into an intricate kata where she fought against a horde of adversaries in a flurry of kicks and throws, keeping up the intensity for several minutes before she collapsed to the floor, sweaty and breathing hard. She looked around and focused her attention on the door to the gym. An offensive odor was wafting in under the door that made her wish she did not have more acute senses than a normal person.

The stench was of rotting flesh and disease. Apocrypha immediately got to her feet.

"Ghouls," she whispered as the doors flew open.

There were five, and they came in a rush, their heads moving back and forth swiftly like they were trying to catch a scent. Then, they focused on Apocrypha. As one, they screamed and rushed her.

Apocrypha allowed them to close the distance between them. When the first one came within reach, she grabbed his arm and swept him to the side, blocking two of his compatriots. She spun to her right, funneling her momentum into a kick to the ghoul closest to her. There was a loud crack as his neck snapped at the impact. Apocrypha allowed herself a smile as the undead monster slumped to the floor. The smile ran away from her face as the one ghoul that still had an open shot grabbed her around the neck, cutting off her breath. A wave of nausea assaulted her as its breath hit her face.

Apocrypha drove her wrists into the underside of its arms, locking them in place, then reversed the movement and smashed them from above, forcing the ghoul to release her. She followed up before the ghoul could react with a strike to its neck, and the ghoul fell back, gurgling blood.

She took a step back to regain her breath. She turned to face the rest just as the three regained their feet and launched themselves at her. Apocrypha backpedaled, trying to evade them, but they were too close. They drove her to the ground, the impact sending stars into her vision. Pain flared through her as one of the ghouls bit into her. She had seen what the aftermath of a ghoul attack looked like. That memory snapped Apocrypha back to full consciousness, and she lashed out, a kick into the groin that sent one ghoul falling backward. Now that she had a little room to maneuver, her hand shot out and grabbed the head of the ghoul to her left, using its eye socket like the hole in a bowling bowl, then smashed it into the one who had taken a bite out of her. Shattered bits of skull from both monsters showered her as their heads collided and splintered under the force of her blow.

Apocrypha slowly got to her feet, pulled the teeth out of her arm, and threw them to the ground, shaking in disgust. She looked up. The last ghoul had regained its feet and was slinking toward the door.

"Gutless. Where do you think you're going?" Apocrypha started sprinting, and as she caught up to the ghoul, she put her shoulder down and intercepted him with a classic football block. He was propelled into the wall just a step before the door. She stood over him with her foot on his neck pinning him to the floor, pondering her next move.

"What the fuck are you doing here?" She spoke more to herself than the monster. Ghouls did not communicate with anyone except their masters.

Suddenly, a scream echoed through the building from the front where the receptionist, Marie, sat. Apocrypha smashed her boot onto the ghoul's head and ran out of the gym doors. The walls were covered in refuse and blood as Apocrypha approached the front entrance.

She turned the corner and stopped dead in her tracks. Around Marie were probably thirty ghouls. They were apparently enjoying Marie's terror, and while she had scratches and bruises, she had no real injuries. Marie screamed again, and the ghouls cackled.

Apocrypha's eyes scanned the room and came to rest on the spot above Marie's desk where the Sin Eaters logo was framed by a pair of matched katanas and a rifle. The rifle was a dud, but the Japanese swords were real, souvenirs from a run against some Yakuza toughs who thought they could kidnap a supervisor from Biotech. Apocrypha ran and leaped, using the shoulders of a ghoul in the back of the mob to propel herself onto Marie's desk. Once there, she pulled the blades from their scabbards and turned using the same motion to sever two of the ghouls' heads from their bodies.

The mob swayed back momentarily at this interruption of their fun but then surged forward. The death of two of their comrades was not enough to influence a group this size. They streamed toward Apocrypha, and she cut and hacked, sending limbs flying as they closed in on her. There was a brief second when she was in the clear, but then the katanas were twisted from her hands as they became stuck in a body. Apocrypha thrashed widely, striking out at every creature that came within reach, but soon, the press of bodies had her stranded against the wall. A ghoul larger and even more disgusting than the rest pressed forward in the mob and leaned in, sniffing at her neck. The creature seemed to consider her odor like it was close to what it was looking for. After a long second, the creature flashed its teeth, apparently disappointed. Apocrypha turned her head, trying to see if Marie had had a chance to get away, knowing that she was dead.

Three shots rang out; the first bullet embedded itself into the meat of her shoulder, but the second two collided with the lead ghoul, its head exploding in a burst of gore. The arms holding Apocrypha relented momentarily, and she shook herself free with a great effort fueled by anger and desperation.

"Fire in the hole!" a voice that Apocrypha barely registered as Kitsune screamed.

Moving on instinct, Apocrypha leaped out of the pile and landed behind the secretary's desk. A moment later, a burst of fire and brimstone erupted in the center of the room, incinerating the mob of ghouls. She thanked the gods that Marie had a combat-rated desk. Apocrypha moved to a sitting position and took long, slow breaths. A moment later, she looked up to find M'rey standing over her.

"Are you okay?" M'rey reached a hand down to help her stand up.

"No." Apocrypha ignored the outstretched hand. "But I will be when I find the fucker who sent those things."

"Okay." M'rey took a slow step back.

Apocrypha regained her feet and saw Kitsune cleaning and bandaging Marie's wounds.

"So, M'rey, tell me again why you don't go on field missions with us," Kitsune asked.

"Because that blast used every bit of my manna, and I will be basically useless for spellcasting for the next twenty-four hours. Also, I want to sleep without thinking of scenes like this. I don't know how you do." He looked at Apocrypha.

"Prayer and lots of alcohol." She sat down heavily on the edge of the desk.

Kitsune walked over and sat next to her, gingerly reaching out a hand to her shoulder.

"Sorry about that."

"You aren't field rated in pistols, and you took that shot. What were you thinking?"

"I figured either way, I was saving you."

Apocrypha opened her mouth to make a comment, then closed it. She couldn't argue with that.

At that moment, Vince's voice burst through the intercom. "Would you guys quit sitting on your ass and get down to the holding cells."

"Gee, thanks, Vince. We are all safe, and we appreciate your concern." Kitsune holstered her gun.

"I don't pay you to be safe, and there are more ghouls in the lower levels."

"Oh, shit." Apocrypha looked at Kitsune, and she pulled her pistol back out as Apocrypha bent down and yanked a katana out of a corpse. They did not say a word but ran for the back stairs.

They sprinted down the steps, heading for the lower levels. The upper levels contained active-duty headhunters, but the lower levels were primarily people who were being made comfortable while waiting to get reclaimed by their corporate benefactors. Apocrypha got to the bottom of the stairwell and waited for Kitsune to get herself set on the side of the door. Then, the pair moved and were through. They took a few steps and stopped; it was over. The floors were slick with blood, and there were gnawed-on dead bodies everywhere. They did a slow walk-through and found the same sights everywhere except for the room where Corey Givens had been staying. The cell was empty of him and of blood.

Apocrypha swiped through the air with the katana and looked at Kitsune. "They got what they came for."

Chapter Nine

Vince called in every headhunter who worked for Sin Eaters, and they spent several hours checking out the building to make sure there were no ghouls still on the premises after searching every nook and cranny. He called everyone to a meeting in his office. Apocrypha had been sent to the sub-basements, and the meeting had already started by the time she arrived.

"About time you got here."

"Nice to see you too, Vince. I am feeling much better after the multiple bruises, breaks, and miscellaneous contusions, not to mention almost being literally eaten while working on your behalf."

"Hey, you knew it was a dangerous job when you took it, so shut up. We have a tier five job to recover him. It's open to all employees. The fee is twice the usual."

"Him, you mean the guy they took."

"Yes, Cory Givens. I know you don't learn their names but

remember his. We must recover him or the bodies of the people who ordered him taken. If word gets out that we can't keep our acquisitions safe until they get picked up, we are out of business."

Apocrypha looked up and did some mental calculations on what she would need to pay the shaman for treating her dad.

"That sounds like it's worth triple." A couple of the other headhunters nodded in agreement.

Vince's face looked like he had gone a week without a bowel movement, but it only lasted a moment. "Fine, but the op is done in one week, or nobody gets paid nothing." He made a grand gesture with his arm and walked away, indicating that the meeting was finished.

Apocrypha was one of the first to walk out of the room. Most of the others present were forming into teams. She started mentally going through the steps she would need in order to find the objective. She never tried to think of them as people. It just got in the way of her doing her job. She took a couple of steps and was brought to a stop by a hand in the middle of her chest. She knocked the arm out of the way and looked up at its owner, who had positioned himself in her way.

"Slagg, keep your hands off me, or next time you'll pull back a stump."

"Shove the tough chick act, Apocrypha. We need to talk."

Apocrypha took a small step back to ensure she had room to move if things got violent. She gave Slagg a quick once-over; he was almost seven feet tall and covered head to toe in muscles and weapons. His face was horribly scarred and had a pair of curving horns on the top; rumor around the Sin Eaters was that he had died, went to hell, and fought his way back out. Apocrypha was not sure the story was far off. He was flanked by Mule, a full-blooded ogre who almost made Slagg look small and handsome.

"What's on your so-called mind, Slagg?"

"You. You need to take a holiday or something and leave this to the rest of us before you trash our reputation more. You screwed up with that witch, and now you lost somebody under our protection."

"Okay, first, I am going to assume you are referring to Novembre's spellcasting and not using that word as an insult and let that go. Two, shut the fuck up and get the hell out of my face. I was not on guard duty when we lost the client. All you really care about is getting me out of the way so you can get more plumb assignments." Apocrypha moved slightly to the side and started to walk past Slagg. He put out a hand to restrain her but stopped short of grabbing Apocrypha as she locked eyes with him.

"I'm not the only one who thinks you're getting sloppy, and none of the other headhunters or even the tech boys are going to give you any assistance. Do yourself a favor and just slink away before something bad happens."

"Slagg, I don't need you, them, or anybody else to complete this mission. And if you plan on finding this guy before I do, I hope you have someone helping you who is smarter than the guy who came up with your codename." Apocrypha ducked under Slagg's arm and walked out of the room into a side hallway. She took a deep breath, looked around, and leaned heavily against the wall. She knew that Slagg was an idiot, but she also knew he made sure to do ops with most of the other members of Sin Eaters and had relationships with them. This was in stark contrast to Apocrypha, who had only done solo missions or with Novembre. She also knew that to complete this mission by the deadline, she would need some tech and research assistance. She ran down a mental list of people who could give her the help she needed and only came up with one.

"Fuck." She smacked her fist into the wall and went to find Kitsune right after she made a stop at the Sin Eater armory.

*

Apocrypha found Kitsune about an hour later in the security office, hunched over a terminal.

"Kitsune, you were at the big meeting. Are you planning on trying to collect on Vince's offer?"

"Why?" Kitsune leaned back from the terminal and looked at Apocrypha sideways without giving her her full attention.

"I was thinking we could work on this one together."

"Like partners?"

"No, not like partners. Like people with interlocking skill sets who want to get paid."

"Sounds like partners to me."

"More like the enemy of my enemy is my friend."

"And the enemy in question is..."

"Vince's bank account." Apocrypha held up a finger. "And if you say yes without busting my balls anymore, I will have a present for you."

"I like presents."

Apocrypha pulled out a large case and handed it to Kitsune. Kitsune opened it. Inside were two Harbinger automatic pistols and two Sin Eater logo pins.

"Wow, guns. I already have a gun."

"What, that .38 that you shot me with? That's a tool for the local gang member; these will get you out of most situations you can get yourself into, and these"—Apocrypha held up the pins—"are miniaturized friend or foe tags. Which means that as long as your..."

"Partner," Kitsune interrupted.

"Associate is wearing one the gun won't fire on them."

"I don't know. It sounds like a gift you would give to a partner."

"If you shut up now, I will throw in some time in the shooting range, teaching you how to dial yourself in dead shot."

"Done. So, what's our first move?"

"You are going to pull video files from the attack and research that Thanatos group we sprung Givens from. I don't know how anyone knew we were the ones who rescued him."

"What are you going to do?"

"I have a street contact who should be able to provide us with some information. I'll call you after I talk to them."

Apocrypha walked out of the building. The first stop she made was to an ATM. She checked the balance and pulled out two thousand dollars, leaving just a few cents in the account. She then hailed a cab.

"Where you heading?" the driver asked.

"The Gate."

"The Gate, you sure? I can point you to a lot less dangerous bars."

"I'm sure."

The Gate was the premier bar and nightclub in the city; it was founded shortly after the return of magic and was the spot where all cultures and races could celebrate together. There were even rumors of portals that could lead you from a bar in one city to a bar in a different city or even country so the night would never end. This fact had made it a hot spot for people wanting to trade information on various legal, quasi-legal, and downright criminal enterprises.

About halfway across town, Apocrypha's phone beeped, and Kitsune's face popped up on the display.

"What's up?"

"M'rey says you're wrong."

"Okay, I'm probably not wrong, and that's not really a way to start a conversation."

"He says those were zombies, not ghouls, that attacked us at HQ. Just for the record, I have no idea what the difference is."

"Quick and dirty, one is supernatural, and one is science-based."

"Okay...wait, that doesn't make sense."

Apocrypha took a deep breath. She really wasn't into having a teaching moment. "What most people call a zombie is what's left after the necrophage disease has run its course. A creature that is living but has no thought but to consume anything and everything in its path. It's a souvenir left by the invaders. A ghoul, on the other hand, is an undead servant—kind of a junior-grade vampire, strong, fast, and willing to do whatever its master says."

"Okay, I follow that, but M'rey says that the nasty monster critters did not trigger the holy symbols around the entrances, so it must have been zombies."

"Yeah, but zombies would not have followed directions. Can you send a copy of the surveillance files to my phone?"

"On their way."

"Kitsune."

"Yeah?"

"Nothing."

"You were about to say good job, weren't you."

"No, I wasn't." Apocrypha disconnected.

Apocrypha spent the rest of the drive wondering what new problem the world had thrown at her.

*

The club was open twenty-four hours a day but was not busy until the sun went down. When Apocrypha entered it, it was just her and a couple of people who looked like they had not seen the light of day in quite some time. There was one notable exception: a tall blond man dressed in well-tailored clothes except for a well-worn leather jacket. He was just making conversation with the bartender, but something about the way he stood screamed cop to Apocrypha. She usually made it a rule not to hang around with cops since they did not like what she did for a living.

Apocrypha sat down at the bar and took a long moment to check out the man. He was good-looking but a little rough around the edges, like the sheriff of a local town in one of the old westerns. He noticed her checking him out and swiveled around in his chair as the bartender spoke to her.

"Greetings, milady. How can I be of service to thee?" The bartender, a tall, tattooed elf, wiped the bar with a rag.

"A cup of coffee, and I need to talk to Crossroads."

"I will get the coffee and let her know you are here, but others are waiting." He nodded, indicating the blond.

The blond turned and reached out his hand. "Roger De Flor, I just got into the city and I'm trying to get a lay of the land. You are?"

Apocrypha started to take the offered hand and noticed the gold sword insignia on the arm of his jacket. She hesitated a moment, then placed her hand on the bar. "Ah, you're one of the new sword bringers. Well, I am nobody special. And the only thing I can really tell you is this is a great place to get a cup of good coffee." She started to tap her fingers on the bar. She did her best to hold her thoughts to herself but just couldn't and continued. "You know it's a metaphor, right."

"Sorry."

"Mathew 10:34. *Do not think that I came to bring peace on the earth; I did not come to bring peace, but a sword.* That was not meant to be taken literally. He meant he was bringing change, not destruction, to the heretics. You guys in The Word always miss the subtle things."

"Interesting, a non-believer who can quote chapter and verse. I am sorry I can't have a competent discussion with you. Questions about biblical scripture aren't really part of my job description."

Apocrypha believed him. Roger was heavily muscled, and she could see the bulge of a large caliber firearm under his jacket.

"I know what your job entails." Apocrypha spoke to Roger, but her eyes were fixed on a place far away and long ago.

"I think we are getting off on the wrong foot here. I just got appointed as force commander here, and all I am trying to do is make contacts with the locals so we can help each other out."

"If you believe what you are saying, then I foresee a large amount of disappointment in your future career advancement. That is not generally how The Word operates around here. However, I will give you the benefit of the doubt and not start hating you just because of your position. Besides, you may not be here for very long. Aren't you like the third guy to have this position in the last five years?"

"Yeah, two of them were apparently not suited for the job, or at least the bishop thought so."

"And the one before that?"

"That was Father Johansson. He was involved in the siege of Chicago, and no one has heard from him since."

"Oh. Sorry to hear that. That was some rough business."

Apocrypha had heard some really terrible things about Chicago. At one time, it had just been a town with more than its share of underworld types, but then something dark and immensely powerful had moved into the Windy City. Almost at once, it had become a Mecca for evil undead creatures in the States. The only normal people left in the city were the servants of the vampires and liches who ruled there; everyone else had been slain.

The bartender waved Apocrypha to come to the back, and she got up from her stool.

"Hey, I did not get your name."

"That's right."

"You know that if you were trying to make yourself forgettable, you just completely failed. I could not forget someone who looks that good being angry at me. It makes me wonder what you would look like smiling."

Apocrypha stopped before going through the door to the back office. "I wonder what The Word's policy on sexual harassment is." Then, before he could respond, she slid into Crossroads' office.

The office was huge, not just big in the usual sense of the world but more extensive than the outside dimensions of the building should allow. It was one of the mysteries of the bar that Apocrypha chose not to think too much about.

Crossroads sat behind a mammoth desk with her feet up, and there was still room for a couple of tables and bookshelves that seemed to hold every book on food and drink ever printed, as well as an impressive collection of vintage guitars. She was an unusual sight, with hair that seemed to shift colors almost constantly. She also had a distinctive accent that, even as well-traveled as Apocrypha was, she could never pin down.

Apocrypha took a chair at one of the tables, judging the distance close enough to talk comfortably but not near enough to be seen as invading her space.

"Ah, Apocrypha, how can I possibly be of service to you? Are you finally going to take me up on my offers? We could really use a touch of the divine around here."

Apocrypha hesitated for a long moment. She was not sure what Crossroads knew and had no intention of giving up any more information about herself than she had to. "I have a job at the moment. I am actually working right now. So just the usual, I need some information."

"I wish someday you would come here for the unusual; it would be such a pleasure to get to know you. Maybe talk about what the future might hold."

For a moment, Apocrypha wondered what might be considered unusual at The Gate. She shook her head and moved on. "Maybe a different time; Vince has got me on the clock. All work, no pleasure, you know."

"Not really, our work is pleasure."

Apocrypha found that the only problem with coming here was that if Crossroads did not feel like getting to the point of a conversation, it could take a while to persuade her to discuss something important. Apocrypha hoped this would not be one of those days.

"Crossroads, I appreciate you taking the time to meet me, especially when you have the new force commander of The Word waiting to meet you." Crossroads seemed to be about to make a comment. Apocrypha rushed on before she could. "So, I will not take any more of your time than I have to. I know I usually hit you up, and a couple of days later, you give me a nudge in the right direction. Vince picks up the tab, and everyone is happy. Unfortunately, today, I am in a bit of a hurry. I am also using my own finances and hope that two thousand will be enough for you to give me something concrete." Apocrypha placed an envelope with all her cash on the table in front of her. This was a big gamble on her part. If Crossroads could not find something, she would be out of options.

Crossroads got up from her desk and leaned forward to pick up the cash from the table. She shook the envelope once and frowned. "This hardly seems like the usual fee."

"Yeah, but I was thinking after the true solstice event?"

"Well, if you wanted to turn that marker in, then I am sure we could work something out, but once it's gone, it's gone."

"I understand."

"Very well then. Go on."

"If you could do everything within your large sphere of influence to help me find the whereabouts of Cory Givens, a cybernetic engineer from Templar Industries, who may or may not have been acquired by a rival corporation. Also, I have some files on some critters I am having trouble classifying that were involved." Apocrypha pulled the storage disc from her phone and handed it to Crossroads.

"We will see what I can find out. Where can I contact you when I get the information?"

"I was going to be staying. The clock is ticking on this."

"A rush job. Okay, do you require any entertainment while you wait?"

"No thanks. I could use another cup of coffee. I would also kill for a three-egg Colorado omelet."

"An omelet? You do know that it is four o'clock in the afternoon."

Apocrypha did not. She realized that her time sense was still screwed up from sleeping for two days. "All I know is that I haven't had a real meal in a long time, and my stomach wants breakfast."

"Well, then, let me get the cooks working on that for you

while I see if I have any friends who might have friends who know your friend."

Apocrypha figured it would be a while before her food arrived, so she put her head down on the table for a moment just to rest her eyes. The next thing she knew, a waiter was at her side, gently nudging her with a plate. Actually, it was not a plate; it was a platter, and the omelet hung off both sides. Apocrypha opened her mouth to ask what species of eggs those were but thought she might not want to know. She had not realized how long it had been since she had a really satisfying meal and dove into the food, so much so that she was only dimly aware when Crossroads arrived a few minutes later.

"That was quick." Apocrypha was actually not sure how much time had passed, just that the majority of the omelet was gone.

"Bad news is always easy to find."

"That sounds ominous."

"You have to promise that either you will not use the information or that you won't get caught. I am not threatening you personally, but if you do get caught and talk about where you got this information, the powers I work for will find all your family members and wreak their vengeance on them. If you get caught and don't talk, you will be dead before we can take any action against you."

Apocrypha's family members, except for her father, were scattered in various far-off places, but if anyone could find them, she was sure Crossroads could. "I won't get caught." She put as much confidence in her voice as she could. She was at once fearful and curious. Rumors said that the Gate was owned by an ancient wyrm, and not much in the world could challenge one of them.

"Both of your questions have the same answer. Your target is being held at the Fae embassy."

"Oh…" Apocrypha's mind raced. That explained a lot. The Fae were a loose association of elves, fairies, and a few other magical races. Unlike a lot of other species, they had never truly disappeared from the world, just grown weaker. The surge of magical power had brought them back to the forefront. They had even taken half of Ireland as their national homeland. They were a recognized nationality, and if you were caught on their land, which the embassy was, they could enact any punishment they desired. It was said that some of the darker Fae gave the gift of immortality to certain victims so they could continue to torture them for hundreds of years.

"Wait, what does that have to do with the ghouls? And why do the Fae want some corporate engineer?"

"The Fae recently reacquired an artifact known as the black cauldron, which brings bodies placed within back to a sort of life. These cauldron-born were the creatures that invaded your headquarters. As to the rest, that is for you to figure out. I have provided all the information I can."

"Well. Crap. Okay, I will take care of it, and no one will know that you provided any information. Maybe if I live, I can even figure out a bonus."

"A bonus for what? I did not give you anything."

"Right!" Apocrypha got up. The adrenaline rush cleansed the torpor that had taken over from the omelet. She pulled out her phone and hit the speed dial for Kitsune, who answered on the first ring.

"Did you feel your ears burning? I was just talking about you."

"What about me?"

"Well, first off, we got some info on those zombies, ghouls, or whatever we killed. They were all recently raised, and they all came from one place."

"Ireland."

"Nicely done. Now, tell me what number I am thinking of?"

"Sixty-nine."

"Okay, that was too easy. Let me try something else."

"Kitsune!"

"What?"

"I am on my way back. Is there anything else I need to know?"

"While I was checking on the ghouls, I got a call to check your references. It was through a couple of layers of contacts, but I think the new Word force commander was checking up on you."

Apocrypha looked over at Crossroads, who smiled sweetly. She realized that she probably traded information about her just as often as she traded it with her. "Well, that is just ducky. What did he want to know?"

"Well, among other things, if you were single. You apparently made an impression, girlfriend. Is he cute?"

"Don't call me that. Yeah, he was, in a religiously intolerant kind of way, but that's not important. Tell M'rey when I get back, I am doing a tier five mage hunt and to pull out and prep my gear. Make sure he packs some spellbinder grenades, and...hold on for a second." She held her hand over the phone. "Crossroads—do you guys still have those T-Rex steaks from that food challenge?"

"Yes, seventy-two ounces each. Why?"

"I'll take two...to go."

"I do not know how you maintain your girlish figure."

"I have lots of near-death experiences." She turned back to the phone. "I also need you to hit logistics and grab me a go-bag and one of my alternate passports."

"Why, where are we going? And what is a spellbinder grenade?"

"A spellbinder grenade is a thing that silences an area, so no spell casting is possible, and we aren't going anywhere. I am just being paranoid in case things continue to go south as fast as they are doing at the moment. Plus, the last thing I wanted was to be on The Word's radar."

"Why do you say that? I mean, I have no love for them, but they are a church."

"Just do what I tell you!" Apocrypha took a deep breath and continued. "Let's just say I have some history. If you want that fat paycheck, I need you to do what I ask."

"Fine, but at some point, we are going to talk, partner."

Kitsune hung up before Apocrypha could respond.

"How you would like your steaks cooked, milady?" Crossroads had apparently summoned a waiter.

"Raw."

"Really?" The waiter raised his eyebrows.

"They are for friends of mine, not me." Apocrypha clenched and unclenched her fist.

"Anything you say, milady."

Apocrypha pulled up the map on her phone to get the location of the embassy. It was on the outskirts of the city, which made sense; the Fae hated being far from nature. She wasn't sure, though; something felt wrong. Tech companies stole experts from one another all the time, but she had never heard of Fae being involved in anything like that. Did this have anything to do with Thanatos Corp's attempted acquisition? Apocrypha did not doubt Crossroads' intel, but she knew there had to be more to this than she was seeing.

Apocrypha started visualizing what she would need to do the insertion when the waiter interrupted her, holding a huge doggy bag.

"I guess this is the biggest item on the to-go menu, huh."

"No, milady."

"Okay...then." Apocrypha went to run her cred stick and hoped there was enough credit left on it to cover the steaks.

Before she could pay, Crossroads nodded to the waiter, and the data pad vanished.

"Don't worry about that; they're on the house."

"Thank you."

"Good hunting; I hope to see you again."

Apocrypha looked at Crossroads. Her tone of voice made her think that Crossroads wasn't betting on her coming out of this okay.

Apocrypha came out of the back room and saw that nightlife had started to come in. The bar was beginning to fill with people and creatures of all sorts. A half-giant stood by the door with a battle-axe that had "complaint department" inscribed on it. Apocrypha gave him a quick salute as she ran out the door and into one of a couple of taxis that always seemed to be parked in front of the bar. The cab driver looked a little disappointed that someone more famous or rich had not gotten in.

"Fifth and Marshal—if you can do it in less than twenty minutes, I'll pay you double." Apocrypha realized as the words came out of her mouth that this might have been a big mistake.

The next twenty minutes of her life was like riding a roller coaster without a restraining device and having people screaming profanity at you while you rode. She got out of the cab feeling more nauseous than she had when she had been hanging in the air outside the window of the skyscraper earlier in the week. She paid him the extra cash and wandered up the steps to the headhunters' central office.

Chapter Ten

Apocrypha stopped abruptly when she spotted Vince waiting at the top of the entrance steps. He always preferred to summon people to his office, and she could not remember a time he had ever come down to meet her. Vince held up his hand as he caught sight of her.

"Stop right there. I need information. Did you find where the target is located and what tier five mage hunt are you preparing for?"

Apocrypha decided to keep it simple. "The Fae embassy."

Vince went pale for a moment. "That changes things."

"What happened to whatever it takes?"

"That was before the Fae were involved. The contract is still open but now it's off the books."

"I'm still going."

"Then I need your headhunter badge."

Apocrypha took a step back. She had never considered Vince

to be a concerned individual when it came to her, but this was a whole new level. The badge marked Apocrypha as one of his employees and as a designated agent of whatever corporation they had been contracted by. It was supposed to mean that if, as an operative, she was captured, then all they could do was hold you until the corporation paid for damages incurred. On most occasions, it just meant an easy way to identify your body after a run went bad. It was kind of a symbol of the street contract: you stay bought, we watch your back.

"You don't think I am coming back."

"If you do this run any way other than complete ghost, Sin Eaters are going to be enemies with the most powerful mages in the world."

"And the richest."

"We are always looking out for new clients, rule number one."

"Vince, you are some piece of work."

Apocrypha pulled the badge out of her back pocket and threw it at Vince. She pushed past him and entered the building. She immediately went to the elevator and took it down to logistics.

The doors opened, and Apocrypha found M'rey standing there.

"You got my stuff."

"I had it." M'rey refused to look her in the face.

"What do you mean you had it?"

"She said she was going to prove herself to you?"

"Kitsune?"

"Yeah, she borrowed your bike and headed for the Fae."

"She is not ready for this; she is... *You let her borrow my bike*?"

*

Kitsune laughed as she hit the throttle on the Lady Shiva. It was the fastest production model motorcycle on the planet, and tonight, it was all hers. She sped through the night toward the outskirts of the city. The elves had taken up residence in the areas around the Cahokia Mounds just east of Saint Louis.

The Fae did things in a traditional method. Their embassy was out in the country and was more like a gothic castle than a conventional embassy. So many of their security measures were old school, but they did include a few new twists. They had placed a minor lightning enchantment on the area around the building that played merry havoc with any complicated electronic device, such as Kitsune's tablet. The device exploded into sparks as she entered the outer perimeter.

The conventional part of the defense was just as it had always been, with archers atop the walls carrying elven bows that were as deadly as any sniper rifle. Kitsune kept her head down as she approached, but no matter how hard she looked, she could not spot them. Kitsune waited for about a half hour, then decided to throw caution to the wind. The walls were rough stone, and it felt surprisingly similar to climbing through the rubble of old Detroit. Kitsune flipped over the wall and found herself alone on the parapet. All the elves who had manned the walls had been rendered unconscious by someone else.

Kitsune leaped down to the ground and started heading for the keep. She was confused. *Could the client have decided we were incompetent and sold the contract to multiple operators?* She hadn't been a headhunter long, but it had happened before with the family. It was never a good thing. About halfway to the keep, she found a pair of red hounds sleeping on the ground. She had seen them in the vids; a red hound was basically a crossbreed of a bull mastiff and an Irish wolfhound, except that through magic and Fae food, they grew to about three times the usual size. They weren't usually bred to be friendly. She was happy that whoever had taken out the guards had also taken care of them.

Kitsune entered the main section of the keep and found a small group of people in emerald and black fleeing toward a glowing portal. Kitsune dropped all pretense of stealth and started running.

"Stop, freeze, cease, desist."

One of the figures broke away from the group and interposed himself between Kitsune and the rest of his group. Kitsune pulled out the pistol that Apocrypha had given her. She had no idea what this guy could do, and she did not want to find out. She squeezed off a shot and missed. She had not trained with Apocrypha yet, but she was usually pretty good at this range. She grabbed the gun in both hands and shot again and missed again—by inches, but still missed. The Fae seemed to smile and made no real attempt to dodge. Kitsune's face twisted in aggravation, and she emptied the rest of the clip. Nothing hit.

"Sorry, lassie, I guess I am just lucky."

"Eat me, Legolas!" Kitsune dropped her empty gun and pulled out a switchblade. Growing up on the streets, she had a lot more experience with a knife than a gun. She leaped and thrust, and the Fae dodged every time, and when he attacked, every one of his blows found its mark no matter how she tried to defend herself. He tagged her several times but never did any real damage. After a few moments, Kitsune backpedaled out of his reach, and he made no attempt to close the distance. She realized he was content just to delay her. She could not think of a way to breach his defenses. All at once, it hit her. She dropped the knife. She took another step and took off her gun belt. She covered the distance between them in quick steps and embraced him with a fiery passion. After several moments, she pulled away.

"Wow." He had a far-off look in his eyes.

"Thanks, you're not half bad yourself, and sorry." Maintaining her grip on his tunic, she slammed her head into his and drove her knee into his gut. He slumped to the ground as she released her grip on his clothes. She could see the rest of his band had gone through the portal, but it was still open, and she started running, hoping to make it through before it closed.

An arrow appeared in her path, then another. She whirled around to see a whole squad of Fae archers led by an elven warrior who was bigger than she had ever seen in any vid. Kitsune realized that, in her excitement, she had taken off running and left her weapons on the ground.

"She is never going to let me hear the end of this." Kitsune dropped to her knees and interlaced her hands behind her head.

"She must be with the usurpers. I saw her kissing Corsair."

Kitsune started to respond, but the huge Fae smashed her in the face, and she faded into unconsciousness.

Chapter Eleven

Kitsune came awake with a start.

"What the..." As her senses slowly came back to life, she could see she was not in a happy place. She was tied to a chair and flanked by four Fae, one of whom looked like he would definitely flunk a steroid test. She remembered him. He leaned down and got in her face.

"You are going to tell us what Nuada is planning, and we might let you live."

"I have a feeling this is going to be a long night. I have no idea who Nuada is."

"Lies! We saw you kissing Corsair."

"Then you also saw me deck him right after that. Tell me there is someone here I can talk to who is not a victim of steroid rage syndrome."

The Fae backhanded Kitsune again. "I have never sampled your human drugs. The Fae come in more sizes than your mind can imagine. I am Tethra, second to Bres, the rightful king of the Fae. And I am the only sight you will see until you give me the answers I seek."

Kitsune looked around the room, trying to see where she was. The place looked like a typical warehouse in the neglected part of town. She assumed they liked to perform their work off-site. It probably made it easier to dump the bodies when they were done, which also lowered the chances of her being rescued.

"Why don't you ask Corsair if I am with his group?"

"He spews the same lies as you. It means nothing. I can ask the questions more strongly if you would like." Tethra pulled a dagger from a nearby table and held it under Kitsune's throat. "I wonder which of your parts you would miss the most." He dragged the knife down her chest.

"You know, I have hung out with real mafia Dons, so it's going to take more than that to impress me."

Tethra slid the knife into the front of her shirt and slit it down the middle, exposing her bra. "We will see how long your bravado lasts."

"Say artichoke if you still have your earpiece in," Apocrypha's voice whispered in her ear.

"Artichoke, artichoke, artichoke!"

Tethra took a step back and looked at her quizzically. "Have you lost your mind, woman?"

"Close your eyes and steel yourself." Apocrypha's voice whispered again. A moment later, the lights went out.

Kitsune sensed movement in the room and felt an impact on the chair she was tied to. She opened her eyes and saw a subtly glowing golden knife sticking out of her arm. The blade had cut the ropes holding her but had not made a wound in her arm.

The darkness only slowed Tethra a little bit, and he turned to face the threat entering the room. He rushed at Apocrypha with the dagger held low. The Fae was quick, and she was barely able to catch his hand as he attempted to stab her. Apocrypha was stronger than a normal person, but one look and she knew that she could not match the Fae. Instead, she introduced him to the Japanese art of aikido, allowing his strength to work against him, and threw him to the far side of the room. He hit the wall and got up without missing a beat. Apocrypha grabbed her dagger out of the chair and slashed off the other rope holding Kitsune to the chair.

"Apollo!" Apocrypha yelled.

"What?"

The last thing that registered was Apocrypha dropping a grenade on the ground. The room exploded in a cacophony of light and sound, robbing Kitsune of control of her senses. Kitsune and the Fae dropped to the ground as the room went from midnight to noon in one second. Apocrypha's shades shifted back from black to normal viewing mode as she gathered up Kitsune's limp body.

"It's been real, folks, but we got to go." Apocrypha rushed from the room, hoisting Kitsune in a fireman's carry. A couple of blocks later, she dropped Kitsune on the pavement.

"Thanks; I can't believe you tracked me down and rescued me."

"Well, when you grabbed my comm gear for the mission, you took a tracking beacon with you. Also, I did not come to rescue you."

"What?"

"Well, first, I went to the Fae embassy, and you know what I found?"

"Some huge sleepy dogs?"

"No. I found a pile of wreckage with my motorcycle's license plate on top of it."

"They killed the Shiva?" Kitsune's face drained of color.

"No, you got the Shiva killed, and when all this is over, there will be a reckoning."

Kitsune stayed silent the whole way back to Sin Eaters headquarters. They immediately went to Vince's office.

"Give me back my headhunter ID," Apocrypha demanded as she walked through the door.

"Did you or Kitsune get identified as a Sin Eater?"

"I did not get tagged, and if you don't remember, Kitsune is still on probation, so you never gave her one. Now give me back my ID. I am not pulling any more of this off-the-book bullshit."

Vince sheepishly put the badge on his desk and leaned back in his chair. Apocrypha thought he might have been trying to get out of her reach. She also thought that it was a good plan on his part.

"What the hell have you gotten me involved with?"

"I told you everything that I knew. You know our motto: if the cash is there..."

"We do not care. Yeah, I got that, but now I am up to my ass in elvish politics, and I need to know something."

"Like?"

"Who is the client?"

"I told you in the briefing, Templar Industries."

Apocrypha rolled her eyes and clenched her fists.

"And?"

"Givens was working on a joint project with them and Saligia."

"Saligia? The people who dreamed up that spider and then let it loose in the sewers to test it. I thought we had talked about them and the fact that I refused to work for them."

"We had, but rule number one kind of trumps all other rules."

Apocrypha pulled Thorn. "Kitsune, hold him down. I am going to finally find out if he actually has a heart."

Vince jumped out of his seat and moved into the corner of the office. "That isn't funny."

"Who's laughing?" Apocrypha took a step around the corner of the desk, and Kitsune moved around the other side.

"Whoa, stop; let's take a second before you do something you might regret."

"Vince, I may face prosecution for what I am about to do, but I don't think I will ever feel regret."

"Listen, I don't know anything about the Fae. I was told a rival corporation called Thanatos took him. They seemed like just another corporation. They had recently signed up for our services, and the background check did not raise any flags. The job was supposed to be a quick snatch and grab. You would never know who was funding the contract."

"Yeah, but regardless of who we snatched him from, how did anybody know that we had him?" Apocrypha twirled the dagger in her hand. "Wait, did you say they had recently contracted with us? You put out an alert, didn't you?"

"That is one of the services that our clients pay for. It's all in the headhunter contract of hire, and besides, it's not like all the things you've done for money have been clean, Apocrypha. I keep some of your secrets as well, so don't get too high and mighty with me."

Apocrypha sheathed Thorn, turned, and walked out of the room. Kitsune caught up to her in a couple of steps.

"So, we still on the job, partner?"

"Don't push it, Kitsune, not now, but yes, we are still on the job. I need you to crack into Saligia's mainframe and find out what Givens was working on. It must be something major to have all of these players trying to collect him."

"Sure, and after that, do you want me to stop by Fort Knox and pick you up some gold?"

"What are you telling me—there are things that you can't accomplish?"

"Saligia and The Word went together and created Apex, the world's premier security protocol. It is an AI-enhanced evolving computer sentinel that adapts to the environment it is placed in and the threats it encounters, and that is the version they let the outside world have. The one on their mainframe is at least two generations ahead."

Apocrypha's face went blank. Kitsune hurried on.

"No, I can't do it. I am an artist at breaking into places and I am rather good with hacking, but I mostly use tools from other programmers and social networking to figure out back doors. To get into Saligia, you would need the equivalent of an arch mage for hackers."

Apocrypha stopped walking. "I might know a guy; he called himself Zero Day."

"How the hell do you know Zero Day? He crashed like twelve hundred systems in one day."

"I caught him."

"You can't be serious. You caught him. How? And more relevant, if you caught him, why would he be interested in doing anything for you?"

"I don't know that he would, but I don't have any other options."

"See what you can get off the Thanatos Industries computers, and I will go pay him a visit."

"Hey, you know, if you want me to make contact with Zero Day, I can. You know, if you want to visit your dad."

"If I want to do what?"

"M'rey said something about your dad being in the hospital, and I thought that…"

"That what? Maybe I should be a good daughter and go sit in the hospital instead of running around here, is that it? Listen, I am doing what I need to do right now. Okay."

"Yeah. I didn't mean anything. I was trying to be…"

"Just mind your own business from now on, if you're capable of doing that." The elevator dinged in front of them, signaling its arrival. Apocrypha hesitated for a moment, then headed for the stairs. "You and me in a small metal box is not really a good idea right now."

"Would it help if I said I was sorry?" Kitsune called after her.

"Doubt it." Apocrypha entered the stairway without looking back.

Chapter Twelve

A pocrypha was still fuming when she reached the Black Adept academy. She paused a moment at the door and took a deep breath. The academy was considered the most powerful mages college in the world and was currently the resting place of the only arch mage/hacker she knew of. Gibson was his name, though he insisted on being called Zero Day. A year and a half ago, Apocrypha had been contacted by a bank and a number of other institutions to find out who had been siphoning funds from their supposed unbreakable computer system. The regular investigators had been having problems finding the culprit. They wanted someone to try some non-internet solution to track the hacker. They had not suspected at the time that it was a fifteen-year-old kid with no formal education in programming who was doing it. He was light years ahead of the curve, and the experts had never been able to figure out how he had done it.

Apocrypha had tried a novel approach; going onto his Face

Space page and just asking him out on a date. Once they had gotten their hands on him, M'rey had indicated he was a wild talent, someone who did magic on an intuitive level and probably never even knew that was where his ability with computers came from. The kid had just been doing it for fun and had not even spent any of the money he took. After Apocrypha had gotten to know him, she convinced Sin Eaters to work out an agreement where he gave the cash back, and the bank did not press charges; in exchange for this, he signed up for a two-year apprenticeship with the Black Adepts and agreed not to touch computers.

Apocrypha was escorted to the library and was told by the school secretary that she would have someone retrieve him from his independent studies. She looked around the room and started thinking that maybe she should hang around after the meeting and do some research. She had never tangled with the Fae before. They were an enormous power in Europe and especially Ireland but did not do much in the States. Apocrypha stood up to head for the shelves when Gibson showed up. She did a double take as he had changed quite a bit in the last two years. He had grown to about six feet tall and had put on a good twenty pounds of muscle.

"Mr. Gibson, or do you still prefer Zero Day?"

"You know you are the only person who has ever called me Mr. Gibson. My parents call me Bill, and now my handle is Zeitgeist."

"Zeitgeist?"

"It means the spirit of the times."

"I know what it means. I just thought..."

"What?"

"Nothing. I am in no place to talk to people about the street names they choose to go by." Apocrypha motioned to one of the chairs across from the table and sat down in her chair.

"I am glad you stopped by. I had actually meant to drop you

a line and say thanks for sending me here."

"Really, that is not what you thought when I dropped you off. I think that place was only barely better than prison to you."

"Yeah, but I have learned a lot since then. I never knew what I was capable of. The trick of talking to computers is the cheapest thing I can do now. Hell, if they let me, I could teach the arch mage a thing or two."

"Well, apparently, being here has not hurt your ego."

"Actually, it did for the first six months. I knew nothing and was pretty much held in contempt by everyone. I was just a minor wild talent who liked computers. Then, I realized that what I did not know was my greatest strength. Magic, even though it just came back, is handled like the people believe it was done in the Middle Ages. The arch mage channels his powers through the four elements. You know, fire, air, water, and earth, something that was proved as just a flight of fancy a thousand years ago."

"It works, though I have seen people conjure a fire elemental, and rooted in truth or not, it still almost singed my backside. That made me a believer."

"But see, that is the essence, belief."

"I heard that before; M'rey said something about the commonly held beliefs of magic providing the framework for what works and doesn't."

"Yeah, but there are forces out there in the collective that no one has tapped into, just waiting to unleash their energies. That is how I manipulate computers. I was raised on video games and movies that said hacking a computer was about fighting things out in virtual reality. So, when I try to enter a system, my magic converts my thoughts instantaneously into the appropriate programs to do what I need."

"Ah, it's funny you should bring that up."

"Hey, I have been good. I haven't even touched a computer." Zeitgeist's face shifted from a teenager trying to look like an adult to a six-year-old kid caught with his hand in the cookie jar trying to look innocent.

"Okay, you still have some things to learn. Like how to lie—you suck at it."

Gibson looked a little sheepish. "It's just been a little here and there to keep up on what's new in tech."

"To be honest, I don't really care. That part is someone else's problem now."

"Okay then, what does bring you to see me?"

"I wanted to know if you would do a favor for me."

"No problem."

"It's the thing I told you not to do anymore."

"Okay."

"It's probably illegal."

"Cool."

"This is supposed to be something you should be hesitant about doing."

"Hey, you could have thrown my ass in jail; instead, you opened my eyes to a world of magic and power. I will do whatever you need me to. Besides, after this, you will so have to go out with me, like you promised."

It gave Apocrypha some comfort that no matter what else changed in the world, apparently, teenagers did not. "I need you to get some information on an engineer named Cory Givens out of the Saligia mainframe. Who he is, what he was working on, that kind of stuff."

"Saligia." His eyes lit up like a kid in a candy store. "Wow, that would be a challenge." He got up, then sat back down again. Then he got up again. "Give me a couple of hours, and I will get you what you need. Oh, by the way, if you see a Saligia strike force set down, it might be wise to deny knowing me." He ran off before Apocrypha could respond.

Apocrypha leaned back in her chair and absently looked around the room. Then her eyes settled on a familiar face. Roger, the new Word force commander. He seemed to feel Apocrypha's eyes on him and turned in her direction.

"Well, Apocrypha, fancy meeting you here."

"Roger De Flor, are you stalking me?"

"We at The Word don't stalk. We seek, and we revel in the beauty that God places in our path."

"And then you burn it to the ground."

"What is it about me that causes you to return my gentle advances with such venom?"

"It's not you; I have had some bad experiences in the past with the church."

"So I had gathered." Apocrypha raised an eyebrow, and he continued quickly. "I mean, your choice of code name by itself says something about your views of the church."

"And you have been checking up on me."

"Just a little; The Word likes to have files on the major operators in the city."

"The Word wanted to know if I was single."

"No, that was me. You know I am new in town, and I never like to date people I work with."

"I am sure the fact that most of them are nuns makes it difficult too."

"There is that."

"So, Mr. De Flor, what are you seeking here? I don't think a minion of The Word would have anything to do with the Black Adepts except maybe to renounce them."

"Minion, really? I think I would be at least a minor despot. Anyway, renouncing things is someone else's department. I am just trying to get a feel for the city. There might come a day when something black and vile crawls out of the sewers, and I might have to ask for help, or there might be students here who might have a future in the clergy. Magic can produce miracles or destruction. I want to be prepared for either."

Roger looked over Apocrypha's shoulder and came to attention. She turned around to see the archbishop of the city flanked by a half-dozen guards.

"Commander, is there a reason you are lollygagging with this woman?" The archbishop's tone was thick with venom.

"I was just talking, sir, trying to keep up with the normal citizens that we are here to serve."

"Oh, I don't think she is one of the people we are here to serve, Praetorian." The bishop looked her up and down. "We know of her and her allegiances. She is just another sellsword. A woman playing dress-up to be sexual eye candy for her corporate suitors. Really, girl, did your mother not teach you any self-respect?"

Apocrypha stood up and looked him in the eyes, her anger building. "So, I guess you are not a fan of the 'judge not lest ye be judged' section of the bible."

The archbishop met Apocrypha's stare with a look that regarded her as nothing less than a cockroach that needed to be stepped on. "I have no fear of being judged. The verse that comes to my mind at the moment is Exodus 22:18: 'Thou shall not suffer a witch to live.'"

The archbishop's comment was the last straw. Apocrypha's body reacted by instinct. Her hand was on her pistol, and it was halfway out of its holster before she had a conscious thought. The archbishop's retinue was highly trained, and as the pistol cleared the holster, six rifles were pointed at Apocrypha. All motion in the library ceased around them as Apocrypha continued to stare at the bishop. The bishop looked smug, confident that his God would deliver him from this threat and that he would see this minor annoyance damned to the fires below. Apocrypha looked into his face. She sometimes got feelings for people just by staring into their eyes, and somewhere deep inside her, she knew that death might be worth sending him from this world. The moment stretched, and Roger slowly stepped in between them.

"Apocrypha, I think this was all just a misunderstanding."

"I don't think so." The bishop and Apocrypha spoke at the same time.

Roger held up a hand and gently reached out for her pistol. "Well, then, how about this is not the time for differences to be settled. Another time, another place, we may be able to come to a better comprehension of each other's role in God's plans. If we all kill one another, then no one wins."

"Fine." Apocrypha started to holster her weapon, and the archbishop languidly held up his hand.

"Kill her."

Before Apocrypha could bring her gun to bear again, Roger turned and was now blocking her from the guard's sights. "Ignore that order."

"You dare to circumvent my authority?"

"Archbishop Carlson, you have absolute spiritual authority. I have absolute authority regarding security decisions, and if you push this moment, I cannot guarantee your safety, so we are leaving." The archbishop locked eyes with Roger, trying to change his mind by sheer force of will, but the commander merely gave a nod to the bodyguards, and they gently began escorting the bishop toward the door. Then Roger turned back to Apocrypha and nodded in her direction. "Ma'am."

Apocrypha watched Roger, thinking he might be an interesting person to get to know if he did not end up guarding the Archbishop of Antarctica's dog. She pushed her gun the rest of the way into its holster and sat back down. She did not know what had happened; she had spent years developing self-control, but she had just snapped when he made the comment about her mother.

*

The rest of the afternoon passed without incident. Apocrypha spent her time reading various books of old lore about the Fae. Based on what Crossroads had said, she found a book about the Black Cauldron. She was asking the librarian if there was any more information about it when Gibson showed up. He looked a little flushed, and Apocrypha wondered if he had heard about her run-in with the bishop.

"Wow, wow, wow." He bounced from one foot to the other like a little kid.

"Would you sit down? You're making a fool of yourself."

"Huh. Oh, sorry, you just have no idea what you are into."

"That, unfortunately, is the story of my life. Would you care to enlighten me?"

"Okay, Givens is a part of the Saligia Technomancer project. Their goal is to combine arcane power with technology."

"I thought that was impossible."

"Technology is just our term for things, not an actual concept. I mean, at one point, Damascus steel was the height of technology, and people enchant those blades all the time. It's like I was saying earlier; it's the belief that holds the key. The people of the world, to a great extent, believe that you cannot combine high tech and magic, and that interacts with the Manna Sphere imposing these restrictions. This guy started out small and was able to combine minor magic with some antiques. He talked about a collection of flintlocks that they were able to enchant with magical properties but were unable to work with current-level stuff."

"So, we aren't getting a magical AR-15, I get it."

"Right, but Cory came up with a plan that is both brilliant and simple. Skip current-generation tech. There are things being developed from leftovers of the great conflict that the general populace has no idea about. It has stuff like nanotechnology that already seems like magic, so the general belief structure does not block it from combining with enchantments. He solved the puzzle."

"So now with that figured out can't everybody create something using those rules? Why kidnap him?"

"Well, first off, I am simplifying the concepts. If you wanted to actually achieve something noteworthy, it would be incredibly complicated. He is probably one of the most brilliant people to come around and it still might take him years for a proof of concept. Second, he had a bad habit of not putting everything in his notes so that Saligia still needed him to work out the bugs."

"Okay, that I can understand, but everything says he was grabbed by the Fae. Why would they want him?"

"That I have no idea. I mean, the Fae might want him to update their current weapons, but more likely, any corporation that is trying to develop this stuff would need the Fae to supply them with raw materials. To do this right, you couldn't use conventional materials. You would need something like mithrium to bond the magic and technology."

"All right, I guess that kind of makes sense. Thanks." Apocrypha got up and started to walk away. She stopped and looked over her shoulder. "When you complete your apprenticeship in six months, call me if you want that date or a job."

Chapter Thirteen

Apocrypha jumped into a cab and headed back to the office. She told the cabbie the address and sat back, saying nothing else until she arrived back at Sin Eaters headquarters. Upon entering, she made her way down to the computer lab where Kitsune was supposed to be doing her research on Thanatos industries. The lab, however, was empty except for a smoking heap where her tablet used to be.

"It's called black ice." Kitsune's voice came from behind Apocrypha.

"What is?"

"A counter intrusion computer program included in some security systems that are designed to kill the hacker. This was a particularly nasty version that almost took me out. It did get my computer, but not before I got this." Kitsune held up a micro disk.

"Is it anything good?"

"Yep. Turns out the CEO of Thanatos Industries, a Mr.

Walton by name, was a hot-shot banker who worked with a lot of mob bosses laundering their money for legitimate enterprises. He was exceptionally good at it. He got arrested a few times but was never convicted. Then he drops out of public life and shortly after that starts a new company, Thanatos Industries, specializing in biotech, cybernetic limbs, and powered armor. They do good work on the power armor, very impressive."

"Maybe we should get some."

"Already did; while I was in their mainframe, I placed an order for some of their top-of-the-line stuff to be delivered to our hotel in Dublin."

"Our hotel?"

"Vince decided that we have already pissed off the Fae, so we should follow the lead and try to recover the asset. He gave me access to the corp card to make travel arrangements. It seems that whatever happened at the embassy spooked Tethra a bit; right after our encounter with him, he took off back home to Ireland."

"And after your last encounter with the Fae, you thought I would want you along?"

"You might need some technical expertise or someone to…"

"Buy me a motorcycle?"

"I did not mean to…"

"Just shut up. I am too tired to deal with any more stuff. You can come, but you do exactly what I say."

"Yes, sir."

Apocrypha frowned but otherwise ignored Kitsune's comment. "Did you find out anything else about Walton?"

"Not that much. He has literally been off the grid for years. No public appearance, not even a picture, but I did see that he made several wire transactions to a numbered bank account that belongs to our friend Tethra."

"So Tethra hates technology but knows what a Swiss bank account is?"

"Maybe that's one of the services that Walton has given him."

"Could be. Well, if he is in bed with the Fae then Walton has to be a bad guy."

"I did some checking on the Fae too. Tethra is the right-hand man for Bres, the legitimate ruler of New Sidhe, which is what they are calling the half of Ireland they took. The old ruler was a guy named Nuada who was attempting to take over the rest of Ireland but, in the last couple of years, had started talking to the humans. There was a big shake-up, and Bres took over. As soon as he did, they ceased all peace talks and called on all members of the Fae court to take whatever actions were needed to throw the humans out of their country."

"So, what happened to Nuada? That was the guy Tethra thought you were working for when he grabbed you."

"He lost his hand in an attack by figures in black power armor. The Fae blamed it on the humans, but nothing was ever proved."

"So, he lost his hand, big deal. Why is he no longer in charge?"

"In the Fae court, only those perfect in form can rule. Nuada lost his hand, and the next in line, Bres, a Formorian, took over."

"Formorian?"

"Dark Fae. Bad guys—actually, I should say worse guys."

"Ah."

"So Nuada stepped down but did not accept Bres as a leader and went off in exile. Apparently, he thought Bres might have somehow been behind the attack."

"Let me guess, the power armor matches that made by Thanatos Industries."

"Yep, but what would Walton be getting from the Fae?"

"They have materials he needs to further Givens's research." Apocrypha replayed her conversation with Zeitgeist and the things she had found out about the cauldron-born.

"So Tethra sent his guys to reclaim Givens from us as part of the deal with Thanatos."

"Looks that way. I guess if we want him back, we are taking a road trip."

Chapter Fourteen

A pocrypha sat in the chair in the corporate jet and shifted uncomfortably in the seat. She hated the loss of control of flying. The idea of placing her life in the hands of someone she had never met before just never sat right with her. She pulled out the material they had been able to garner on the current state of Irish politics. When the magic had come back a lot of species and creatures had started popping up that had not been seen in the world for millennia. Some of them came as changelings, unusual creatures that were born to normal parents, but the elves basically revealed themselves. They had used what little power they had left to hide from the eyes of man, but with the surge in magical power that came from the creation of the Manna Sphere, they had been able to come back to the world in force. Almost at once, they had started conflicts with man, and after a couple of years of warfare, they were awarded a portion of Ireland as their new homeland.

There were still isolated incidents that disrupted the rest of

Ireland's economy. A corporation had come in and taken over running the non-elven half of Ireland. The CEO styled himself a new high king of Ireland and wanted to retake the rest of the country. There had been a series of small-scale conflicts on and off ever since then. Lately, things had begun to change. The elves, though powerful, were few in number, and they started to accept normal humans who came in as workers and merchants. Those humans were treated as second-class citizens, but New Sidhe offered a haven for people wanting to escape from the corporations and technology that were starting to slip into every part of life. This influx of people had made the current ruler more amicable toward humanity, and he had started to have talks with the High King about opening trade relations between the two sides, that is, until he was removed from office. After the change in rulers, the attacks on the western half of Ireland by elven separatists started up again.

This conflict allowed Apocrypha and Kitsune to have an excuse to enter the country. The High King had a group of power-armored knights called the Lia Fáil, named after the sacred stone in Ireland, who were tasked with dealing with the separatists. Saligia had arranged for the pair to visit with samples of next-generation technology to improve the Lia Fáil and hopefully convince the High King to aid them in recovering Mr. Givens. Apocrypha had doubts; anyone who called themselves a High King in this day and age probably had some issues, but he was the closest thing they had to a friend in the country.

Apocrypha flipped the overhead light off and closed her eyes, willing herself to sleep.

She woke to the sounds of the stewardess asking them to get ready for landing. She looked at her watch, an old pocket watch that her father had given her, and adjusted the time to the current time zone. Kitsune looked at the watch like it was an alien artifact but kept silent.

The plane landed, and Apocrypha got up and straightened her gear. Kitsune started to get up as well, but Apocrypha held her hand up.

"Let's let everyone else get off first."

"Okay, can we get some kippers for breakfast?"

"What the hell is a kipper?"

"I don't know. I heard about them in a Supertramp song and always wanted to try them."

"Sure, right after we pump the High King for information on elven separatists trying to kill him, we will ask for kippers."

"Cool."

Apocrypha leaned back against the chair, allowing the other passengers to pass by, and closed her eyes for a moment. She briefly considered smacking her head against the wall. As she opened her eyes again, a piercing note echoed through the plane, and she clamped her hands to her ears to block out the sound and pain. Apocrypha ducked her head to look out of the window and saw a woman flying in the air. She had a ghostly complexion, and as she screamed, the passengers collapsed all over the tarmac.

"Kitsune, we have to..."

Apocrypha looked down at Kitsune and her eyes were rolling back into her head. Apocrypha could feel the scream starting to sap into her spirit as well. She assumed that her heritage was giving her some protection from the banshee's powers, but it was fading fast.

"Sorry, I have to borrow this." She grabbed Kitsune's music player and pulled on the headphones, cranking the volume as high as it would go. The blazing guitar riffs of Within Temptation at eleven seemed to drown out some of the scream, but it was still only a matter of time. She jumped over bodies in the aisle of the airplane and made her way to the door. As Apocrypha exited, the banshee saw her and smiled.

"I am Death Knell, and Bres sends his greetings." The pitch of her scream changed, and Apocrypha leaped to the ground out of reflex. The place where she had been standing was engulfed in a wave of sound, destroying that section of the plane.

"That's a new trick."

The banshee swiveled her head in Apocrypha's direction, and she leaped again. The banshee tried repeatedly, but each time, Apocrypha was a half second in front of the attack. The banshee rose higher into the air, a frustrated look on her face, and screamed again. She returned to her first pitch, but this time, it seemed directed just toward Apocrypha. The scream drowned out the noise of the music from the player.

Apocrypha stopped in her tracks. She clenched her teeth and reached into her back pouch for the anti-mage gear she had packed for the trip. She pulled a spell blinder grenade out of her pocket and took one determined step, then another. The banshee smiled and flew toward Apocrypha. As it drew nearer, the scream's intensity increased, driving her to her knees. The banshee's smile widened until Apocrypha triggered the grenade, and silence descended upon the area. The grenade was designed to create a null zone of sound to prevent wizards from casting spells but canceled out the banshee's attack as well.

Death Knell's eyes went wide, and she seemed to be trying harder and harder to vocalize.

Apocrypha looked up at Death Knell, taking a moment to enjoy the creature's sudden reversal of fortune. She used the motion of getting to her feet to drive more power into her punch. The blow impacted the banshee squarely in the jaw, and she went right down. The creature slumped to the ground in a heap. Apocrypha spit on the ground.

"Yeah, that is what I thought."

Apocrypha turned to see Kitsune slowly getting out of the plane.

*

Apocrypha and Kitsune spent the next two hours sitting on the tarmac, waiting for the appropriate authorities to show up. The local police were not up to speed on dealing with the Fae and were waiting for the High King's security group, the Lia Fáil, to arrive and take possession of Death Knell. When the Lia Fáil finally made an appearance, it was obvious. They had a military-grade helicopter, and as it landed out strode five guys in power armor with a Celtic motif emblazoned on it and one young woman.

She was towered over by the men in the power armor, but then again, she would probably have been short next to almost anyone. The way she carried herself, however, left no doubt she was the lead badass of the group. They were all strength and posturing; she was death on a short chain. The men were bodyguards, but Apocrypha got the strong feeling she was the assassin. The lead Lia Fáil came forward to meet Apocrypha, while the young woman ignored Apocrypha and Kitsune and went straight to Death Knell.

"About time you guys arrived. I have been waiting for hours."

"I am sorry, miss. There has been a rash of Fae attacks today. Including one that resulted in..."

The Lia Fáil stopped in mid-sentence, and Apocrypha looked over to see that the young woman had silenced him with a look. The Lia Fáil hesitated to speak and instead nodded to the young woman.

"Look, whatever happened to you guys probably had something to do with what happened here. Either we can get in the Fae's way, or we can get in each other's way."

The young woman seemed to consider this for a long moment, then made a brief nod to the bodyguards. She got up and headed for the chopper while one of the Lia Fáil picked up Death Knell. Apocrypha started to follow, and the Lia Fáil she had been speaking with put a hand on her chest. She gazed up into his face plate.

"Unless you are planning on buying me dinner, take your hands off me."

"This is official business of the state of western Ireland and..." He stopped while he appeared to be listening to a communication, then turned to look at the chopper the young woman was hanging out of. "Badb says to get your stuff and be quick about it."

"Hey, Kitsune, we're leaving."

Kitsune stood in the middle of a group of police officers making small chat and fending off requests for her phone number.

"So, is this the whole enemy of my enemy is my friend thing?" Kitsune asked as she caught up to Apocrypha, walking to the chopper.

"I don't know, but we'll find out soon."

The pair climbed into the helicopter and, after a moment of looking around, sat down in the doorway with their legs hanging out. The chopper had been gutted to fit the Lia Fáil's power suits, but there was still no extra room. Apocrypha pointed out some straps to Kitsune for her to hang on to and gave the thumbs up to Badb. Badb nodded to the pilot, and the chopper surged into the air. The flight was quick, and soon, they landed near what appeared to be a Gothic cathedral. As they got closer it was obvious that it had been modified with current technological security measures. Badb led Kitsune and Apocrypha into the heart of the building and the insides had been entirely made over into a modern corporate structure. Badb pointed to the stairs while the Lia Fáil continued into what looked like a series of holding cells.

The stairs went quite deep into the earth, and when the group arrived at a steel door, Apocrypha assumed that they must be several levels under the building. Badb bent down to have her retina scanned, and the door opened. She went inside and took a seat at the head of the table.

"So, how can you help me?" Badb began the conversation.

"Besides taking care of a banshee that was killing your citizenry."

"That would be something you did for the Lia Fáil. I have a different set of responsibilities."

"I just bet you do." Kitsune dropped loudly into the first seat she came upon. "You seem to be the queen of badass around here, but the Fae are getting their hands on some game-changing equipment. So, you want us to get it back and leave, don't you?" She put her feet up on the table and leaned back.

"That is something you could do to help me."

Apocrypha looked over at Kitsune and raised an eyebrow. Kitsune taking the lead was unexpected, but she decided to let it go. She preferred the tactical part of the job and could let Kitsune handle some of the talking stuff.

Kitsune laid out most of what had gone down since they first got the assignment and ended with, "Now we need to find Nuada."

"Finding Nuada is something that pretty much everyone in Ireland has been trying to do since Bres got crowned. At this point, the alliances are still shifting in the Fae; I couldn't even tell you who is on his side."

"I know one person who is. A guy named Corsair, six-two, dark hair, very lucky." Kitsune gave an abbreviated version of her last encounter with the Fae.

"I am impressed. Most people don't survive their first encounter with the Summer Court. You must be incredibly lucky."

"Yeah, that's how we feel, lucky," Apocrypha interrupted. "Would you know where we could find Corsair? Is he still being held by Tethra?"

"By chance, I do." She picked up a remote from the table and flipped on the TV. She scrolled through a couple of menus and pulled up a video. "This was recorded earlier today." The screen was filled with an image of people setting up for a significant event. She turned up the volume. "The Fae are gathering at Corcaigh, what was once the city of Cork, and where they have set up a large arena on the remains of the city railway station. There, Bres will officiate over the execution of an unnamed Fae who was convicted of treason against the crown. There have been many demonstrations against the coming execution, some of which the Fae guards have disrupted using force." Badb flicked off the TV. "Our sources tell us that the person they are going to execute is Corsair."

"Well, once we have rescued him, he will be sure to take us to Nuada."

Badb looked at Kitsune like she had grown a third head. "I know that after your defeat of Death Knell, you might be thinking that the Fae are just like the street toughs and corporate security you deal with, but they are not. You would be crazy to think you can just stroll in there and take Corsair."

"She is crazy, but we don't have any other options. They said the arena used to be a railway station. Couldn't we use the tunnels to get in unseen?"

"Maybe, but all the power has been cut off to that side of the border."

"So, if we do go in, can we expect help from you?"

"No, the High King has forbidden us to take direct action against the Fae until things get sorted out. If we marched across the border, it would be open warfare again. The best I can do would be to give you an opportunity for some reconnaissance. The Summer Court is having a party tonight to celebrate the coming execution as we and the Court are nominally at peace at the moment."

"This is peace?" Apocrypha interjected.

"Bres indicates that he cannot control the actions of all Fae, and some independent operators occasionally take action against us."

"So, until you can prove it, he can deny it."

"Yeah, but as I was saying, since we are not actively engaging in hostilities, he sent an invitation to the party. We were going to ignore it, but you could go as my representative and maybe get some intel for your raid."

"Or we could use it as an excuse to walk through their wards and kick the shit out of them."

"No, you couldn't." Badb spoke softly, but her voice caught Kitsune and Apocrypha's attention. "If you do that, then the accord will be broken, and the war will begin again. Worse, you would have insulted their honor, and they would be bound to slay every man, woman, and child in western Ireland."

Apocrypha smiled. "Fine, I will play nice, but if they raise their hand to me, then all bets are off."

"Tethra will not break the truce because if he did, then Bres would have to take action against him. The party is in a couple of hours. I will have you brought to your hotel and get someone from protocol to send you something suitable to wear."

"Suitable?"

"It's a formal event; think one part Renaissance fair and one part black-tie dinner."

"Thrilling." Apocrypha rose to her feet.

"Cool, can we keep the clothes?" Kitsune smiled as she joined Apocrypha on her feet.

"Oh, and one more thing," Badb said as Kitsune and Apocrypha were about to walk out of the door. "Don't mess with Bres's stag."

"Is that some sort of euphemism?" Apocrypha raised an eyebrow.

"No, the Fae have spent years using magic and breeding to bring Irish elk back from extinction and the herd is his prize possession."

"Ah, okay, the deer are off limits."

"They are a little more than just deer; they stand about two meters tall, and their horns are about four meters wide."

"Ah, okay, the nightmare deer are off limits."

Chapter Fifteen

Apocrypha had just stepped out of the shower and was wrapping herself in a towel when Kitsune barged in.

"Clothes are here."

"Oh, happy day." Apocrypha walked out and found two large bundles of clothing on the beds. Kitsune was holding up two of the outfits, looking like a kid in a candy store. She immediately pulled off the jeans and T-shirt she was wearing to start trying things on. Apocrypha walked over and slowly went through the items that had been left for her. They were all in different shades of floral color and adorned with bows and frills. They reminded her of a time when she had been hired to work security at a wedding, and her cover had been a bridesmaid. She held a couple of dresses up to her body, looked in the mirror, and threw them down in disgust.

"Nope, not happening. There is a chance I might die tonight, and that is not happening in chartreuse."

Kitsune looked over, standing in a stylish designer dress, all black with hints of pink that matched the streaks in her hair. "Hey, they can't be that bad."

Apocrypha picked up a long lavender dress that looked like someone had killed a couch to make it.

"I guess maybe they can be."

Apocrypha pulled on a pair of jeans and reached for her sweatshirt. "They do not make clothes for an athletic woman who is six feet tall. They just don't. Which is fine. I don't mind shopping in the guys' section; their clothes hold up better. I am going to wear jeans and a T-shirt." As she was speaking, she pulled the hood off her sweatshirt and pushed her sleeves up to her elbows. The sweatshirt shifted as she pulled and tugged, changing shape.

"What did you just do? You a fashion mage or something?" Kitsune stared at Apocrypha.

"Huh? Oh, the sweatshirt was a gift from a mage I used to run with. It is supposed to keep me magically undetectable, so to let me wear it all the time, she included an enchantment that lets it change to become whatever kind of clothes I want."

"That may be the coolest thing I have ever heard of. How far can it go?"

"I don't know. I usually just switch between a black hoodie and a black T-shirt."

"You have the ultimate power, and you're wasting it on T-shirts." Kitsune ran across the room, grabbing her tablet as she went. She pulled up a search and found a white chiffon dress. "Try that."

Apocrypha looked at her. "Why?"

"Try it!"

Apocrypha took a step back. She closed her eyes and took hold of the fabric of her shirt, imagining the dress. When she opened her eyes, she was now dressed in the white chiffon dress.

She looked in the mirror, and her reflection did not look like her. Except for the wedding assignment, she had never worn a dress.

"Holy crap, I might have to kill you and take that." Kitsune's squeal broke Apocrypha out of her reverie. Kitsune was flipping through pages of images of dresses, trying to decide what to do next.

"Wait, go back one."

"Okay."

There on the screen was a Victorian-style dress in black lace; it was elegant and feminine without being silly. Apocrypha reached out and touched the screen gently, and the chiffon dress shimmered and reset itself into a mirror image of the outfit.

"Wow, nice choice, kind of a gothic fairy godmother from hell, but on you, it works. Now you just need to start putting on your face."

"What do you mean?" Apocrypha was transfixed, looking in the mirror.

"Makeup, you need to do your makeup."

Apocrypha looked at her quizzically. "I'm not going to wear any makeup."

"You are not going out in that dress without makeup. How do I put this? It would be like pulling your gun without the bullets." Kitsune looked at Apocrypha, who appeared to be unsure of herself for the first time since they had met. "Just sit down and let me get my tools."

Kitsune gently pushed Apocrypha into a nearby chair and grabbed her makeup bag from her bed. She pulled another chair close to Apocrypha's and started working. They sat in silence for a while, but as Kitsune started on Apocrypha's eyeliner, she looked deep into her eyes. "Can I tell you a secret?"

"For some reason, I am hesitant to say yes."

"It's not about my internet history or anything like that."

"Go ahead."

"Makeup is not for the boys, it's not for the world, it's for us. It is a chance to accentuate, to hide, to say this is how I choose to be."

"And what if I choose not to wear makeup?"

"Then that is a decision you make for yourself and lets you define yourself. But if you don't mind me remarking, it doesn't seem you have had a moment to pick your relationship with the stuff. There you go, all done." Kitsune swiveled Apocrypha's chair to face the mirror.

Apocrypha looked into the mirror and just stared. Then, a single tear rolled down her face as unfamiliar feelings filled her.

"Hey, hey, none of that. Crying will ruin your mascara. "Kitsune dabbed at Apocrypha's face. "You know we are going to get through this just fine. I mean, we already took on ghosts and abominations. How tough can a couple of elves be?"

Apocrypha took a deep breath, and her voice quivered a little as she began to speak. "I am not afraid of them killing us. I've never been afraid of dying. It's just not in me." She turned to look at Kitsune. "Did I ever tell you my father used to kick my ass? I don't mean like he used to beat me for being bad, even though that happened too. I mean that in everything we did, he treated me as a foe to be defeated from like the age of five. He wanted me to earn my victories, so there was no taking it easy on his kid. I had to know what it felt like to take a beating and then get back up for more. I had to know exactly how long it would take a broken arm to heal. I had to know what it might be like to wake up in the middle of the night with a two-foot poisonous spider in my bed. I almost wish I could hate him for it. But it was all he knew to do, and I am okay with it; hell, I am probably still alive because of it. But then I look in the mirror and see this. I see a woman who could have gone to prom, a woman who gets asked out on dates instead of to provide cover fire, a woman who could have a family. I see my mom." Apocrypha gripped the arms of her chair and gently rocked back and forth.

"Your mom?"

"Everybody keeps asking me what I am. I am a Nephilim."

"A what? Is that a kind of changeling?"

Apocrypha cleared her throat. "'The Nephilim were in the earth in those days, and also after that, when the sons of God came in unto the daughters of men, and they bore children to them; the same were the mighty men that were of old, the men of renown.' Chapter and verse, so to speak. The TLDR of it is basically way back; there was a little divinity introduced into my bloodline. One of the side effects is that we become hyper-focused on things. My mom wanted to be an ambassador, so her gifts let her sense emotions, learn a dozen languages, and other things. None of them protected her when they came for her. My dad decided that was not going to happen to me, so I got boot camp at age five. I never got to choose."

Kitsune gripped her shoulder. "You know where I learned to do all this makeup and stuff? My mother taught me. I started out as a thief in the ruins of old Detroit, but then, as they worked on new Detroit, my mother started directing me to new places. She would make me up and dress me in the finest clothes she could find to go into bars and get guys to take me to their hotel rooms so I could rob them. She would say whatever it took to get the goods; of course, whatever it took was never taken from her. But I have chosen to take those lessons about makeup and use them for my purposes. I think our pasts mean that we have to decide who we are for ourselves, and that family has nothing to do with blood."

Kitsune reached around and hugged Apocrypha.

A sudden knock at the door startled them both, and Apocrypha jumped up, grabbing her gun off the table.

"Who is it?"

"It's the hotel concierge. The limo will be out front in about ten minutes for your use, courtesy of the Dagda Corporation."

"Thank you." Apocrypha looked at Kitsune, her face once more composed. "I'm going to take a walk. I'll meet you at the car."

Kitsune watched her walk out, then whispered. "Okay, partner."

*

The limousine pulled up to the event, and Kitsune and Apocrypha got out. They walked to the front door, where Tethra and a few guards stood. Apocrypha handed him the invitation, and he smiled at her. Then he looked at Kitsune, and recognition came into his eyes.

"You!" He then took a second look at Apocrypha and recognized her as well. "So, the fates have delivered you to my doorstep."

"Yes, and we accept your invitation of guest status and pledge to do no harm to you or yours as you pledge to harm neither me nor mine while we partake of your hospitality."

Tethra fumed. By tradition, he could not attack them without bringing dishonor upon him and his liege lord. "Enjoy yourself as if this was one of your last nights upon this world." He stepped back and allowed them to enter the great hall.

*

Four hours later, Apocrypha kicked the door open into the hotel room, carrying Kitsune in her arms.

"I can't believe you almost threw up on the Morrígan. She is the actual embodiment of vengeance around here."

"It's not my fault. The mead was a little spicier than I thought. But it was really good. Can we go back and get some more?"

"No!"

"Listen, it's not my fault. I was just matching how you were drinking. I am sorry."

Kitsune looked like she was going to throw up again, and Apocrypha raced to the bathroom. She placed Kitsune in the tub and turned on the shower.

"What the fuck!"

Kitsune leaped to her feet. Apocrypha always took super cold showers, and she had apparently forgotten to change the water setting. Kitsune stood there in her lavish dress, which was soaking wet and now clung to her body, hiding nothing. Apocrypha's breath caught in her throat. She was not prepared for the effect seeing Kitsune like this would have on her. She had been with lots of people before, both men and women, but there had always been a detachment with their couplings. She enjoyed it but never so much that it drove her to want to stay over and cuddle. She looked slowly over Kitsune's body, and all she could think of was spending an entire weekend in bed. She shook her head violently to clear her thoughts. It was like the conversation she had had with Kitsune had unlocked feelings she had been denying.

Apocrypha walked into the bedroom of the suite and slammed the door. "Get a hold of yourself."

"I'm so, so sorry. I did not mean to embarrass you. You're my..."

"Don't say partner," Apocrypha called through the door. For some reason, that word suddenly had more weight and power than it should.

Kitsune staggered back. "I'm just going to sleep on the couch."

"Yeah, do that." Apocrypha laid back on the bed. She closed her eyes and willed herself to sleep but it took several hours.

Chapter Sixteen

Apocrypha woke to the sound of noises coming from the other room of the suite. She figured Kitsune must be moving around. After last night, she was not sure what she was going to say. She cracked the door open and peeked out. Kitsune had several cases open and was busy laying out a bunch of armor components. She had some sort of high-tech helmet on her head. Then Apocrypha realized why she had woken up. There was a Pomeranian-sized mechanical spider crawling across the bed toward Kitsune. Kitsune seemed blissfully unaware. Apocrypha looked around; most of her weapons were across the room. So, she quietly reached out and took the Gideon bible off the dresser. Then she sprang and brought the book down onto the spider, smashing it.

"What the hell are you doing?"

"That thing was going to attack you."

"No, that is a remote-operated drone. When I saw that Thanatos had them in spider forms, I just had to pick up a couple. You just smashed about two hundred thousand worth of tech."

"How was I to know? Besides, spiders creep me out a bit."

"Spiders creep you out? After all the shit you have encountered?"

"I had a bad experience with a spider, okay."

"What happened?"

"I said *I had a bad experience with a spider.*"

"Hey, watch the volume, okay. Still recovering from that Fae mead. Tell me, did I do anything bad or cringe? I kept most of my clothes on, right."

"Yeah, your clothes stayed on the whole time. No story to tell." Apocrypha looked around the room, not wanting to make eye contact.

On the floor were five or six more spider drones scurrying everywhere. Apocrypha raised her foot.

"Don't! I will put them away if you just let them live."

Apocrypha slowly lowered her foot. "So, do you have anything that isn't creepy over there?"

"Absolutely; allow me to introduce you to the Thanatos person defense system Mark V. The basic armor is upgraded Kevlar with titanium composite plates to protect the most critical areas. A helmet with a full communications suite and enough buckles and bows to hold any weapon you might like to bring to the fight." Kitsune held up a sheer black fabric. "And for the pièce de résistance, we have the Thanatos Reflex protection system Mark I. The armor is composed of nanotech that is pliable and form fitting until it senses a high-powered impact approaching and then turns into a highly resistant form of protection."

"Cool. How are they against magic-wielding enraged elves?"

"They seemed fairly effective against Nuada."

"True."

Kitsune put down the nanotech armor and looked at Apocrypha with a serious expression. "So, did I at least provide enough of a distraction for you to place a homing beacon? I hate to think we came all this way just to get lost."

"Yeah, you did that."

"So, any thoughts on how we are going to make our entrance?"

"Well, they are apparently expecting trouble. They have guards at all the entrances and not just guards but the Fae Royal guard. There are also expected to be a couple thousand people in attendance. Bres wants to make an example of Corsair. That's good for sneaking in but really cramps our style for getting out. We can probably use the tunnels to get under the ceremony. Badb says there are still some working train cars. I figured we blow our ceiling/their floor, grab Corsair, and run like hell."

"Run like hell is our plan."

"I try not to make things too complicated."

"Well, at least it's a plan," Kitsune said as the nanotech weaved its way up her form. "So how do I look?"

"You look good." The nanotech armor was form-fitting, and Apocrypha tried to be flippant, but she just did not know how to talk to Kitsune at this point. She had shared more than she had with anyone in a long time, not to mention the effect Kitsune's body was starting to have on her.

"Thanks; I would hate to be out of fashion for my funeral."

"Well, at least we are in Ireland. There is no better party than an Irish wake." Apocrypha forced herself to smile.

She put on the rest of the armor and started filling every holster and pouch with as many guns and ammo as she could. Kitsune was doing the same and even had her spider drones carrying explosives and detonators.

"Do we have to bring the spiders?"

"Now is not the time to be hating on the spiders."

"It is always the time to hate spiders, but it is fine to bring them if you think they will be useful."

Once the two of them were all packed, they went downstairs and found a truck waiting for them, another present from Badb. They drove to the last train station before the border and entered the tunnels. The power to the tunnels stopped as soon as they passed under the border. Large signs warned the pair that they were entering the Fae-controlled side of Ireland.

After a couple of miles, they came upon a train engine car that was still in reasonably decent shape and attached a portable generator to it. Once they got the train going, the ride to Corcaigh was pretty quick, and using the tracking device, they were able to navigate the railways.

"Hey, can I ask you a question?"

Apocrypha looked up from monitoring their path. "We have started asking permission?"

"I know I say a lot of shit before thinking. It's part of my charm, but I try not to be a total bitch."

"What is your question?" Apocrypha kept her face passive.

"Who was it that killed your mom?"

Apocrypha took a deep breath and let it out slowly. She opened her mouth once, twice, and on the third time, she found her voice. "It was agents from The Word."

"What the fuck. Let's go end those fuckers. I knew there was a reason I hated those uptight motherfuckers."

Kitsune's instantaneous reaction brought a slight smile to Apocrypha's face. "The people who did the deed are no longer with us. It was the first live-action operation my father sent me on. It was a present, he told me, for my thirteenth birthday."

"Oh my God. Elisheva, I am so sorry." Kitsune leaped up and hugged Apocrypha.

"It's okay. That was a while ago." Apocrypha pulled out of the embrace and held Kitsune at arm's length. "What the fuck did you call me?"

"Elisheva, Vince's files said that was your given name."

"You hacked my files."

"I did it the day I found we were going on the first operation. I did not really know you."

Apocrypha looked deeply into Kitsune's eyes. She wanted to be angry, but it had been so long since she had shared secrets with anyone that she could not hold on to her anger. She released her grip on Kitsune's shoulders and did not resist as Kitsune hugged her again.

"The Nephilim are something of a problem for the church. They basically put us in one of two categories: a tool to be used or a demon to be destroyed. My mother did not like being used." Apocrypha steeled herself and gently broke herself from Kitsune's grip. "But we have to keep our focus on the fight in front of us. But when this is done, I get to read your whole file."

"It's Matilda."

"What?"

"My name, it is Matilda."

Apocrypha started laughing and almost doubled over.

"It's a family name."

"Okay." Apocrypha turned away to hide the fact that she was still laughing.

*

About an hour later, they arrived at what was once the train station. Kitsune put her bots to use. They scurried up the walls and set the explosives in just the pattern that Kitsune had designed.

"Do I blow it now?" Kitsune's hand rested on the detonator.

"We want to make sure that we wait till almost the last minute to make sure they have the least chance to react. I figure once the ceiling comes down, I will be able to make a dramatic entrance and free Corsair. Then, hopefully, his luck will keep him alive long enough for us to get back to the train. Then, assuming the train is faster than the Wild Hunt, we make it across the border and start on the next leg of the journey."

"If you say so."

"Okay, I know what will probably happen. Every warrior will turn on us in a race to see who gets to kick our ass first. But at least if all else fails, I get another shot at Tethra. Especially after the shit he said about you at the party."

"Wait, what did he say about me?"

"It's just about time." Apocrypha nodded at Kitsune.

"I said what did he say about me?"

Apocrypha gave Kitsune a stern look.

"Fine. But this discussion is not over." She flipped open the trigger to the detonator while Apocrypha pulled her forty-fives.

Kitsune held up her hand and counted down from five to four, three to two to one. A series of explosions sounded on the roof in rapid succession. Then, nothing. Apocrypha turned and slowly looked at her.

"What the hell happened?"

"They must have magically reinforced the floor."

Apocrypha smashed the butt of her pistol against the wall and started looking around wildly before turning back to Kitsune.

"Hey, don't give me that look. I used as many explosives as I could without guaranteeing that the whole tunnel would collapse.

Let's get back on the train and get out of here. I am sure they heard us."

"What about Corsair?"

"What about him? He's a big boy and made his own decision to be in this whole Fae civil war thing. We'll have to figure out another way to find Nuada."

Apocrypha looked up at the roof again. While it had not collapsed, there were a few places where sunlight showed through, some even big enough for a person to slide through. She remembered from the party last night that the Irish elk pen was not far away from the execution site. A small smile played on her lips.

"I don't like that look."

"Get in the train and take it a little way down the tunnel and get ready to go. I'll be right back." Kitsune opened her mouth to try to talk her out of the plan. But one look at Apocrypha's face and she realized it would be pointless. "You are one crazy bitch."

"Thanks." Apocrypha climbed on top of the train car and leaped for the ceiling. She grabbed the edge of the rubble and pulled herself up. Kitsune looked upward for a long moment. She knew there was no way she could follow, so she entered the train car and started to move it down the track.

Apocrypha climbed out onto the surface and took a slow look around. A large crowd had gathered around the dais where Corsair was tied up but none of them seemed to have noticed the rumbling from the explosion. She took a moment to orientate herself, then headed due west where she remembered Bres's pride and joy awaited.

She breathed a sigh of relief when she got to the pen. There were no guards. She assumed that the wrath of Bres was enough to keep most people out. A large runestone kept the elk locked up and pacified, but her Thorn made short work of that.

"Hello, nightmare deer, don't mind me." Apocrypha rushed to the back of the pen and vaulted onto one of the elk. She grabbed a fistful of fur on the back of the beast's neck and emptied her pistol into the air. Nothing happened.

"God damn fucking Fae." Apocrypha reached down to her belt. She had two explosive grenades but had hoped to use them during the actual fight that was coming. She figured she had no choice. She set the timers for five seconds and tossed them to the empty rear of the pen. A moment later, an explosion rang out. The animals as one surged out of the pen. Apocrypha was rocked backward and barely managed to stay on top of her mount. The whole herd shot straight toward the dais. There were at least a hundred of the beasts, and they were not stopping for anything. They crashed into the crowd, and the whole place erupted into chaos. The elk streaked through the ceremony, heedless of who or what they ran into. The guests did everything they could to avoid hurting the elk, even if it meant taking a shot from their antlers. Apocrypha let her mount follow the rest of the pack until she reached the dais. She leaped off and rolled on the ground as the beast passed by it.

Directly in front of her was an altar with Corsair along with Tethra standing with a large axe. Tethra was screaming obscenities and yelling at people to restore order when he spotted Apocrypha. She blew him a kiss and sprinted over to the altar. He leaped off and met her halfway, bringing the axe down in a double-handed grip. She raised her pistol and Thorn to block the attack. The pistol shattered, but Thorn held, stopping the blade from entering her body. The impact still drove her to the ground. He reared back and attacked again, forcing her to roll to her left then to her right. She dodged his next strike and kicked him in the groin. He staggered back for a moment but otherwise seemed unaffected. The moment was all it took for her to regain her feet.

"I guess they were too small of a target for me to hit."

A look of blind hatred appeared on his face, and he charged Apocrypha again. He was single-minded in his pursuit of her, attacking again and again with a blood-chilling fury. She blocked and dodged. The whole time, a portion of her senses was attuned to the chaos around her. She took a backward leap to get some distance between the two of them and sheathed her knife. Tethra stopped short for a second, then rushed at her, just as an elk leaped over the dais and impacted him, sending them both falling to the ground.

Now that the way was clear, she ran up onto the altar and sliced through Corsair's bonds. He looked up at her and seemed unable to focus. Apocrypha assumed he was either drugged or enchanted or both. She picked him up and slung him over her shoulder in a fireman's carry. Then she turned to leave but was stopped dead in her tracks as a large sound boomed through the air, and a mountain of dirt erupted around her. She took off at a sprint toward the place where she had climbed up and found instead that the elk had reached the weakened floor where they had placed the explosives and collapsed the whole thing. The only problem was a large contingent of the Fae had recovered and now stood between her and the hole.

The royal guard started to advance. They were a varied sort, some large and some small, but all looked like they were eight kinds of deadly. They began to form a loose semi-circle to avoid getting in one another's way when they rushed her. The lead Fae took a step forward, then the world erupted in bright light. The auto dampeners in the Thanatos helmet kicked in. Apocrypha was only blind for a moment, but the Fae were startled and thrashing about. Standing between Apocrypha and them were three Fae dressed like the royal guard but with intricate masks on. Apocrypha moved slowly, edging her way closer to the hole. She had no idea who they were, but she was not assuming they were friends just because they were against the other Fae. The leader of the new Fae made a couple of gestures, and a shimmering barrier of light erupted between the royal guard and the hole. The mage stepped back and allowed one who wore an exceptionally gilded mask to advance. As he stepped forward, Apocrypha noticed that he only had one arm. He was between her and the edge of the hole, but she had a good guess who he was.

"Nuada, I presume?"

"Yes, milady. I don't know why you chose to make our cause your own, but I welcome your aid. This will be a glorious battle."

Apocrypha could hear the royal guard beating on the magical shield and knew that it was coming down soon.

"You know, that does sound fun, but how about an alternate plan." Apocrypha adjusted Corsair more securely on her shoulder and planted a kick right into the chest of Nuada, sending him sailing into the crevice. A moment later, she followed, leaping downward. Apocrypha landed awkwardly but unhurt, her fall cushioned by the many elk already at the bottom.

Nuada picked himself off the ground. "You go too far, lady. Were this a different time and place, I would answer your assault with my blade. As it is, I forgive you, but I will run no further." Nuada's two supporters landed next to him. They were braced for a fight.

"Listen, you great ass. You may live in a fairy tale world, but I risked my life in the real world to save your friend and to meet you. You want to have an honorable and stupid death, fine, but choose a different day. We get out of here; we regroup, and then you pick a time when your death will mean something and not just be an example of how Bres has everything under control."

Nuada's supporters pushed past him and started to move forward at this sign of disrespect. Apocrypha dropped Corsair onto the ground and pulled her other pistol. She leveled it at the mage, thinking it was probably best to take them out first, but waited. They stopped but did not seem intimidated, more like waiting for the go-ahead to kill her.

"Solstice, please seal the hole. We are leaving."

Solstice turned without looking at Apocrypha and made a ritual gesture, and the earth surged upward, blocking the royal guard from following them for the moment.

"Magus, take care of Corsair." Nuada fixed his gaze on Apocrypha. "Few in any realm have ever talked to me like you have. You will have to answer for that someday. I assume you have a way out of here."

Apocrypha pointed down the tunnel and started walking. "Kitsune, I am on my way, and I have some friends."

The group moved quickly and soon climbed onto the train and were speeding back to the border.

"Nuada, Solstice, Magus, this is Kitsune."

"I am charmed, milady." Nuada actually spoke like he meant it and made a formal bow work while hurtling in a jury-rigged train car. Magus and Solstice stood, not relaxing a moment. Corsair let out a loud snore that seemed to break some of the tension.

"So, Apocrypha, can I ask why you choose to rescue Corsair? This is not your affair."

"Well, it could be because he and Kitsune go way back, but I would be lying. This is one of those enemies of my enemy is my friend things. Your pal Bres has been working with humans to try and integrate technology and magic. I think you have already encountered their first shared project. They kidnapped a researcher to help them, and I was hired to bring him back. I figured if I got Corsair, I would get to you, and you would get me to him."

"I had not pegged you as a mercenary."

"Not everyone is royal born; bills have to be paid."

"That is true. I was not making any judgments; you just have the feel of a higher power around you. Well, that is neither here nor there. Bres did make an alliance with some humans. He used them to get me out of power and he hopes to use them to bring the oldest Fae back to this world. There are some creatures that even Fae fear, and after the last civil war, they were sealed away to another place, and all agreed they were too dangerous to be let free to roam the world. Bres has been having your scientist working on a way to crack those doors and allow them to enter so he may expand his empire."

"You know, at some point, I would like someone to tell me something that makes me think the situation is going to get better." Apocrypha began pacing in the small railway car. "I thought that Bres had just kidnapped the researcher as part of a deal with an American."

"I think that is how it started but Bres has a nose for finding things he can twist to his own use."

"All right, well, let's head back over to the other side and figure out our next move." Nuada's guardians glared at Apocrypha again. They seemed to be running out of patience with Apocrypha's tone toward their lord. Apocrypha went to the back of the train and sat down, trying to let the adrenaline seep out of her system. Kitsune followed her back and offered her a shoulder. She leaned over and closed her eyes without thinking about it.

Chapter Seventeen

A bout an hour later, the group walked into the hotel lobby.
Apocrypha was impressed that the hotel staff did not bat an
eye when a group of heavily armed and otherworldly creatures
walked by. He just smiled and asked if more towels would be
needed. They took the elevator up to the room. Kitsune held up
her hands to Apocrypha as they entered, signaling that she was not
getting involved in the drama. She flopped down on the bed and
flipped on the TV.

"Well, the good news is that this means the scientist is still
in Ireland. I guess our first order of business is to find out where
he is located and get him away from Bres."

"No, he's not." Corsair sat up; apparently, whatever Magus
had done had finally allowed him to recover. "Before Tethra
brought me to be executed he bragged that they had succeeded
with the human's help, and they were able to summon Balor."

"What's a Balor?" Apocrypha turned around because

whatever show Kitsune had turned on was making a racket. "Kitsune, will you turn that down?"

"Hey, I never knew there was an Irish equivalent of Godzilla. Check this movie out. The special effects are really good."

Annoyed, Apocrypha took a quick glance at the TV. The screen showed a giant with a single eye walking through the streets, smashing everything in its way. A feed under the scene indicated that this was not a movie but a news broadcast. The commentator announced that there was an evacuation order covering the area where the hotel was located.

"Is that a Balor?" Apocrypha pointed a finger at the television.

The blood seemed to drain from Corsair's face as he looked at the TV. "Well, I guess that answers that question. Bres did not waste any time sending the big guns after us."

She turned to look at Nuada. "Is there anything different about Corsair?"

"No, what do you mean? He is the same person as always. He is not under a charm or glamour if that is what you are asking." Apocrypha scowled at him, and he relented, giving Corsair another look. "He is wearing a new cloak. I guess Tethra wanted him to look good for his execution."

"Or he hoped someone would try to rescue Corsair, and if they were successful, then Balor would know where you are."

"Oh, that is why it was so easy for you to rescue him."

"Easy...fuck you. Fuck, Tethra was so big and ugly I never even thought he might be smart." She grabbed the cloak off Corsair's shoulders. "Kitsune, we have to go." Apocrypha grabbed a spare pistol and some clips and shoved them into the pouches of her armor. Then, she hastily scribbled a number on the hotel message pad. "Nuada, call this number and tell them you have a message for Badb from me. Tell her that I am on my way to her house with a very big problem not far behind."

"This is not your affair. You should let me and mine handle it."

"I'm with him. Balor does not look friendly," Kitsune chimed in as she grabbed her gear.

"Nope, if you show up at Badb's door, the Lia Fáil will most likely open fire. They are the only people I can think of who can handle this thing."

Apocrypha threw a chair through the window and took a running leap out toward the roof across the street. This part of the city was congested, and the alley was not wide, so she easily cleared the distance. She rolled as she hit the ground and kept running. An impact behind Apocrypha let her know that Kitsune had followed her. Off to the left, she could see Balor's head peeking over the smaller buildings.

She had thought that Tethra was the biggest, ugliest Fae in the bunch, but this guy made him look insignificant. She continued to sprint across the rooftops. The monster was moving slower, but his size and strength let him bully his way through the buildings in his path. Apocrypha kicked it into high gear; she did not want to take any chances with Balor catching up. She looked down at the cloak in her hands. Bres must have used an electronic tracking device so that Nuada's mages would not notice it. Hell, it had fooled her as well. She was used to dealing with magic or tech but not people who used both.

Apocrypha reached the citadel and was joined a moment later by Kitsune. Kitsune collapsed to the ground, breathing heavily. "That's it. I am taking up jogging when we get home."

As they stood at the fortress door, two large attack helicopters came over the walls.

"I guess they got the message."

Balor took the moment to make his entrance. He toppled an apartment complex as he came, barely noticing the damage he had inflicted. The two helicopters took parallel positions and opened fire with machine guns.

"Yeah, get some."

Balor shrieked as the bullets pelted his skin. They opened up wounds, but those same wounds healed almost instantly. He roared his defiance. He then opened his one great eye, and a beam of mystic energy shot out. He swept his head from left to right, and everything in its path, including the two choppers, was obliterated.

"Oh, shit."

"Yeah, what you said." Kitsune pulled out her pistol. "Not sure what this little thing can do, but maybe we can blind him." She ran toward Balor, leaping and cartwheeling across the square.

"Kit, no, we have to run."

Apocrypha ran after Kitsune. She was only a moment behind, but Kitsune used that time to cross the distance. Balor smashed his fist down upon the ground. She dodged the blow, then used it to vault at his face, firing wildly the whole time. She floated in the air for a long second. Then she was caught. The monster had her in his grip and slowly squeezed. Because of the nature of the attack, her armor failed to activate at all, and she screamed in agony.

Apocrypha dropped her guns and pulled out Thorn. Throwing herself forward, she caught hold of his sleeve. She pulled herself up onto the arm that held Kitsune. She sliced downward into the engraved bracer he wore, and the metal parted like butter before her blade. She stabbed deep and severed the tendon going to his hand. He flung his arm upward, releasing Kitsune and sending both of them flying in opposite directions. Apocrypha watched in horror as Kitsune sped toward the ground. Before she hit it, a black and green blur interrupted her fall and took the impact.

Apocrypha landed hard on the ground, seeing that Badb had caught Kitsune. She shrugged off her discomfort and got to her feet. As she moved, Balor focused on her, and she realized that the giant was still keying in on Corsair's cloak in her pack. She wanted to run to Kitsune's side, but she knew the farther she got away, the better off Kitsune was. Apocrypha turned and ran down the street; before her, a bus turned on the avenue, and she vaulted to its top. The bus suddenly surged forward, and she had to put her hands down to steady herself. She assumed the driver must have gotten a look in his rearview window. She was hoping that Balor would not utilize his eye beam again. But she knew if he did, she was dead, so there was not much point in worrying about that. Up ahead in the square was a building marked as being set up for demolition. Apocrypha figured that would be as good a place as any to make her stand and leaped off the bus.

She reached the parking lot in front of the abandoned building, which was empty except for a crane and wrecking ball. She looked around for anything she could use as a weapon to affect a creature that big.

"Why is there never a howitzer around when you need it?"

A moment later, the sun was blotted out, and Apocrypha dived to the side more by instinct than design; a Lincoln town car impacted the ground where she had been standing. The impact sent shrapnel flying everywhere. A piece lodged itself between the armored plates protecting her legs. She composed herself for a moment, then pulled the metal out and screamed. She had felt a lot of pain before, but this was going to go in her top ten. She pulled the cloak from her pouch and started to wrap it around her leg, hoping to staunch the bleeding.

"Sorry, I need that." Before Apocrypha even knew Badb had appeared she had grabbed the cloak and started sprinting toward the building. Balor walked by Apocrypha like she was not even there and continued his dogged pursuit of the cloak bearer.

Badb ran about thirty yards and entered the building. Apocrypha realized that any more running would only put innocent people at risk. This would have to be the place to make their stand. Balor surged forward with focused intent and smashed its hand through the wall of the building, then withdrew it a moment later, blood flowing out of its palm where Badb's long sword had cut a deep gash. Balor reared back and smashed its hand into the third floor, and the process was repeated. The cuts were only doing incidental damage and while they were succeeding in keeping Balor occupied, they were not a real threat.

Apocrypha wondered how long Badb could keep it up. She looked around, and her eyes fell on the demolition equipment, which gave her an idea.

Balor grabbed the front of the building and ripped the façade clean away, revealing Badb standing with her bloody sword. She was defiant but looked tired. She looked over Balor's shoulder and saw Apocrypha climbing into the cockpit of the wrecking ball. A slow smile played across her face. A moment later, the floor she was standing on collapsed. The monster advanced on the Irish operative.

"Hey, asshole!" Apocrypha screamed at the top of her lungs. Balor ignored her entirely and raised its fist. Apocrypha frantically worked the controls, sending the wrecking ball into the monster's knee and driving it spinning sideways. She fumbled with the machine, bringing the ball backward for another swing. The creature turned around, moving slowly due to the damage to its leg. The monster was just starting to open its single eye again when the ball hit again directly into its face, caving its skull in.

Apocrypha climbed down from the crane and walked across the parking lot; Badb met her halfway there. She bent down and wrapped the cloak around Apocrypha's leg wound.

"We should be safe to use it for this now."

Apocrypha nodded her appreciation and started to hobble down the street back to the Lia Fáil citadel. She could hear the sirens of the emergency responders coming to the scene. Her mind flashed back to the sight of Kitsune falling, and she choked for a moment. She tried to hurry up, but with every step, pain shot through her leg. Badb and Apocrypha got back to the fortress just as they were lifting Kitsune into the back of an ambulance. Apocrypha rushed to get into the ambulance as well. Badb put a hand on her shoulder.

"Wait, let them go. If you go, they are going to have two people to worry about. Let's get your leg bandaged up. Then I will drive you to the hospital."

Apocrypha turned with hatred in her eyes then she softened. "You're right."

She shut the door to the ambulance, and they drove off. Badb whistled for an EMT to come over, and Apocrypha sat on the ground so they could check her out.

*

After about an hour, Apocrypha joined Kitsune at the hospital. Kitsune was in almost a full-body cast with only her head visible and was heavily sedated. Apocrypha stood at the door and looked for a long time.

"I hate hospitals." She walked slowly to the chair next to Kitsune's bed and stared at her. One of the doctors started to say something, but Badb whispered in his ear, and he walked away.

A couple of hours later, Kitsune had still not moved. Apocrypha looked at the clock, then over to the door, and Nuada was standing there. She seemed to skip the steps of getting up out of the chair and was just across the room, slamming him into the wall. She had one of her pistols in her hand and pointed at his head.

"You bastard, she wasn't even part of your little war."

"I regret her injuries, but she is not here because I involved her. I believe you did?"

The hammer of the magnum pulled slowly back with a click. "What did you just say?"

"You very recently told me to think clearly. Do the same. I did not invite her to Ireland. I will have my people do what they can to heal her, but you do not get to blame this on me."

Apocrypha stared into his eyes and slowly released the hammer.

"I know I am the one to blame. Well, I am going to sit right here until she gets better. Then I am taking her home." Emotion choked her voice.

As she slowly walked back to the hospital bed, Kitsune made a slight noise. Apocrypha rushed over and leaned close.

"Why are you still here?"

"I'm by your side."

"But you still have a job to do."

"Not anymore. I am going to hang out with you. I will find another. Fuck Vince and his job."

"That's not what I mean. That's not your job. You get between bad people and good people. The ally to the Fae is a bad guy; you need to take care of him."

"I can't leave you. Not now."

"Badb will take watch over me. She's just like you without the nice parts. But it's not her place to finish this. It's yours."

"But..."

"Go."

Apocrypha had tears in her eyes. She gently took Kitsune's face in her hands and kissed her. "Okay, partner." She turned to look at Nuada. "I need two favors."

"What do you need?"

"I need a set of mithrium chains and an address."

*

A couple of hours later, Apocrypha was sitting on the edge of an elegant four-corner bed in an elaborately decorated room. She had not taken Tethra for someone into the baroque style, but its artistic merit was not the first thing they had disagreed about. It had taken a while, but she had gotten into Tethra's personal abode quietly and now was looking down at Tethra sleeping. She thought for a brief moment about just killing him, but there were larger issues. Three boxes of sleeping pills in his evening ale had made it surprisingly easy to restrain Tethra with the mithrium chains. She pulled out a flintlock pistol she had borrowed from the high king's collection. She leaned over Tethra's body and put the barrel against his knee. The gun went off with a loud boom.

Tethra did not scream in pain or rage; he simply glared at Apocrypha with hatred in his eyes as he strained against the chains. She did not say a word; she just slowly and meticulously reloaded the pistol and placed it against his other knee.

"So, I was doing some research into the Fae. You know what you guys hate: cold iron. It turns out cold iron is just unprocessed metal, like the kind they used in musket balls." She fired again.

Again, Tethra made no noise as the pistol went off.

"I am beyond torture; do your worst," he said after another couple of moments of testing the strength of the chains.

"I know you are. I am not going to torture you. That was just to make sure I had your attention and maybe for a little personal satisfaction." She reloaded the flintlock and placed it against his groin. "I do have your attention, right?"

Tethra glared at her.

"I'll take that as a yes." She pulled a stack of photos from the pack and threw them across the bed. They were all images of Tethra meeting with various elements of the Lia Fáil, starting with Badb and ending with Nuada himself. Tethra's brows knotted together in confusion.

"Isn't it amazing what you can do with a little time and Photoshop? I know you are thinking you can proclaim your innocence, and I am sure that Bres is in a forgiving mood at the moment. I mean the whole Balor dead, Nuada still free, and all of it your fault hasn't made him the slightest bit angry."

The determined look that Tethra had when he thought he was going to be facing torture started to fade a little.

"You know, I figure that the reason you were not worried about me torturing you was that the Fae have far worse punishments. You're probably right, which is, of course, your problem right now."

"I will never betray my king."

"That's fine. I could not give a rat's ass for this civil war you have going on. I need the name and location of your partner in America. It's not like he's Fae, and you already got what you wanted from him." Apocrypha looked at Tethra. As she watched, the wheels began turning in his head. After a few moments, his eyes went to his desk, where there was a large stack of papers. She got up and on the top of the pile was a personal correspondence from a Mr. Walton of Thanatos indicating they should deliver Mr. Givens to him at his home in Chicago after the scientist had completed the gateway. She folded the paper and put it in her pack.

"Pleasure doing business with you." Apocrypha waved at Tethra as she went to the open window she had used to gain entry.

"This is not over. We will have another meeting," Tethra growled from the bed.

"You can bet your ass on that." She slipped out of the window and into the night.

Chapter Eighteen

" **J**umping out of a perfectly good aircraft is not a natural act."
Apocrypha repeated the phrase over and over as she looked
out of the helicopter. She had done many things, but base jumping
was not something she did often and not usually from an aircraft.
She adjusted the wingsuit for what was probably the hundredth
time.

"We're almost over Chicago. Also, your boss is on the line."

Apocrypha closed her eyes and counted slowly to ten. She
put the offered headset on. "What is it, Vince?"

"I just want to make sure you know how important this is."

"You really think calling me and telling me how important
this job is to our clients is going to help me right now? This is about
more than a job now."

"No, I meant it is important that we show you can't endanger
headhunter personnel without facing repercussions."

"Vince, you aren't getting sentimental on me, are you?"

"No, if it gets around that people can hurt Sin Eaters with impunity, it's going to cost me a lot of money in workers' compensation. That is it."

"Vince, for a second there, I almost thought you had a heart."

The line went dead. She stopped trying to talk herself into the right frame of mind, turned, and leaped out of the plane.

*

Chicago was the heart of darkness in the United States. Shortly after the magic returned during the great conflict, undead and supernatural forces began to return to the world. The mafia families embraced them, trading their souls for unholy power, and they centered their power in Chicago. As the years went by, they consolidated their hold. The Dons who had become liches at this point joined their power and created a veil of everlasting darkness over the city. After that, it did not take them long to throw out any challenges to their power. After a couple of attempts, even the federal government gave up on ousting them and instead provided funding to the Church of the Word to contain them.

The church was mostly successful, but the city had still become a haunt for people and criminals who would risk anything to escape from the law. The sad fact was most of them just ended up becoming sustenance for the underworld. The fact that her quarry had chosen to live there for the last two years made Apocrypha wonder who she was dealing with.

She allowed herself to free fall, gathering speed until the towering buildings of Chicago came into view. Then she opened her arms, allowing the air to fill the slots of her suit, transforming it into a wing that allowed her to glide on the wind currents.

She swooped into the city, the air whistling past her. The experience was a rush, and she lost herself in the moment. Then, she was brought back to full attention as a loud howl overrode the wind.

"Fuck," Apocrypha cursed. She had thought she would have more time before she attracted undead attention. The blood taint that creates vampires does not always work the way it does in movies—sometimes, you do get Eurotrash with a lisp who is just as likely to talk you to death as to suck your blood. Sometimes, you get a Vrykolakas, a barely human, mostly bat-like monstrosity who flies through the night seeking nothing but to feed its hunger. Their existence was the reason she had chosen not to do a traditional parachute jump into the city. She pulled her arms in a little tighter and hugged the outline of the buildings. Risking a look back, she saw the creature falling behind when from around the next corner, there appeared another one. She attempted to swerve, but the suit failed, not being up to such a quick change in direction, and the creature hit her; instantly, its talons were tearing at her armor and her pack. The collision knocked her to the side, and she hit the glass windows of the skyscraper, shattering them, and crashing into a collection of cubicles within. She rose slowly; the beast's claws had shredded her armor, but it had least saved her from being cut to pieces by them. The impact had her moving slowly as she tried to take stock of what she still had on her. She shook her head to clear it. A moment later, the Vrykolakas crashed through a window and came straight at her almost before she could blink.

She barely dodged the first attack and grabbed a filing cabinet. She used it to bash the creature on the side of the head. The office furniture smashed into the Vrykolakas and shattered, doing no real damage. She took a quick stock of her options and ran.

The room was large and full of leftover cabinets and furniture from when it had been part of the city's business district. She weaved and dodged through the cubicle maze while the Vryko-lakas waded through anything in its way. This allowed her to stay a few steps ahead of it. As she approached the back of the office, she kept looking every which way for an exit. As she ran, she was confronted with a choice of stairs or elevator. On pure instinct, she propelled herself toward the elevator; maybe she could lose the beast down the shaft. She ran and pulled Thorn from the sheath nestled in her back. She always felt a little more confident with it in her hand. The blade burned with a fiery light as it always did in the vicinity of the undead and she felt a little of the fear of Vryko-lakas fading. She jammed the blade in between the elevator doors and sprung them open, only to find herself face to face with the elevator and not an empty shaft.

"Motherfucker."

She turned to head for the stairs, but her time had run out. The monster impacted her frame, and she heard the armor shred, giving up any protection it once had, accompanied by a shower of blood. She did not feel the slash, which meant she was probably already in shock. She thrust back with her dagger, now glowing white hot, but she barely caught the beast. The wound she inflicted sizzled, and the Vrykolakas hesitated for a moment, caught off guard by the sudden pain.

She realized she wouldn't have much more of a break and took the opportunity to dash into the elevator and leaped for the access door to the shaft. She skipped opening the door and just crashed through, pulling her torso into the open air of the shaft. She enjoyed a brief moment of freedom; then, it grabbed her foot. She responded by ramming her other foot into the ugly mass that passed for its face once, twice, and finally, on the third time, it released her. Apocrypha pulled herself on top of the elevator car and grabbed the cable, using all her strength to dig into the metal underneath the years of slime and grease, then sliced the cable length directly under her hand.

The car hung in midair for a long moment, then it plummeted. The claw of the Vrykolakas reached out of the access panel, but it was already on its way down. The building rocked as it impacted the ground.

She hung for a moment on the cable, waiting for some sound that would mean it had survived, but nothing came. She took a deep breath and sheathed her dagger. She took a moment to gather herself, then swung on the cable back into the business office. She landed hard, her legs giving out under her. Reaching back, she felt around the remains of the ceramic plate that had protected her spine, and her hands came back covered in blood.

She stripped off her armor because it would not be of any use at this point and used what was left of the base suit to create a makeshift bandage. She had a med kit in her pack, but that was now somewhere on the streets of Chicago, along with her guns. She was down to Thorn, a few clips of ammo, and her cell phone. Not that she had anyone she could call. No matter what Vince said earlier, he was not going to send any backup. Apocrypha gathered her strength and regained her feet. The room spun for a moment, and she steadied herself on a desk. The injuries were nothing she had not healed from before, but it would take time and someplace safe to rest, neither of which she had available. She saw the sign for the stairs next to the elevator and made her way over. The stairs were what her old track coach would have called a good, honest workout, the kind that made you question your commitment to the sport. As she went down the steps her mind went back to what Kitsune had said and whether it was true. Was her calling truly protecting good people from bad things? She had certainly gotten tired of the perpetual gray world of corporate intrigue.

On the other hand, she liked eating and having a place to live. Kitsune, why had she kissed her? That had not been on her mind; it just seemed like the right thing to do. Thinking of that moment put a smile on her face, and she realized she would like to kiss her a lot more. She slipped as she reached ground level, and pain shot through her back.

"Get your head in the game, woman." Thinking of Kitsune, as pleasant as that might be, would just be a distraction. A distraction that could get her killed.

She took a quick inventory of her wounds. The bleeding had stopped, but the cuts felt hot to the touch. She was not sure if it was just a fever or if the Vrykolakas had injected venom into her body. She peeked into the lobby to make sure none of the Vrykolakas were still looking for her.

She took a deep breath and walked out into the street. The streets were mostly empty, though there were parts of the city that still had light and power. The underworld seemed to enjoy some of the trappings of civilization; it was just the sun they had chosen to abandon. She found a corner and orientated herself to the map she had memorized before making the journey. She was in luck. There was a place she could take shelter in for at least a brief time, and it was only a couple of blocks away.

The trip took far longer than it should have, as Apocrypha did her best to stay out of sight of the Vrykolakas in the sky and the roving bands of ghouls on the streets. That, plus the increasing pain from her wounds, made it slow going.

The Holy Name Cathedral was quite a sight, even after all that the city had been through. It was the largest Catholic church in Chicago, huge and shaped in a classic Gothic style. She had been worried that city inhabitants would have torched it, but it seemed untouched by all the darkness around it. As she climbed the few steps in front, she found the doors had been boarded shut from the outside. It took her a few moments, but she was able to wrench the planks off the door and gain entry.

The church was vast and gloomy and was quite different from the places Apocrypha had gone for mass when she was young, but she still felt a little better inside. The fact there were examples of faith and light the underworld could not wholly destroy gave her a little hope. She had no hope that the building was still sanctified. She knew she should explore the church or, at the very least, put some of the boards up on the inside to keep the beasts at bay. But as she walked down the center of the pews, a profound fatigue settled on her.

She climbed onto the altar and lay back; a stray thought popped into her head that Father Raphael would be yelling at her if he saw her. She sat back up and lit the candles around the altar. It would probably not mean anything, but it gave her a small amount of peace as she lay back.

"I guess it is possible for even me to have a little blind faith." Her eyes closed, and consciousness faded from her.

Chapter Nineteen

Apocrypha woke with a start. She scanned the room, wondering what had triggered her senses since it was still a couple of minutes before dawn. Then she remembered that dawn would not be coming.

She slowly sat up but did not feel any of the aches and pains that she should have. The fever was gone. She removed the makeshift bandage, and the wounds were healed. She reached under her shirt to feel for the crucifix she always wore. She found it and grabbed it tightly. It was cool to her touch.

"Okay, so did not get turned into a vampire." She looked up into the rafters. "Thanks?"

It might seem strange, but Apocrypha had never believed in miracles. She got off the altar feeling anxious. She was used to relying on herself and was not sure what to make of this latest development. But she did know she felt more rested than she had since her father had gotten sick, and that was worth a lot. She dipped Thorn into the holy water basin by the front door as she left, not even wondering how it was still full.

She exited the church and found herself in the middle of a climactic battle. There were bodies of ghouls strewn about the street, and a lone warrior in sword bringer regalia was engaged with two more.

"The Word on my side now; things are getting really weird."

He was very skilled and appeared almost inhumanly strong and fast. She knew that the Church of the Word had outfitted some of their agents with body armor that enhanced their abilities, but this was more impressive than she had ever seen before. He was good but left his back open, and a third ghoul circled in behind him. She was not sure where he had come from or why he had decided to be her guardian angel, but she could not let him get taken down. She raced forward and grabbed the ghoul by the scruff of its neck, pulling the beast up short. The sudden force from behind sent it crashing to the ground. She plunged Thorn into its heart.

The sword bringer glanced momentarily over his shoulder as if checking to make sure she was doing her job properly, then leaped into the air and severed both ghouls' heads from their shoulders with a sword that crackled with energy. He landed on the ground with his weapon extended and slowly looked around to see if any other threats existed, then got up. He gave Apocrypha a long once-over.

"I knew that something in the church was worth protecting when the candles were lit, but I never expected someone like you."

She eyed him up and down. She could tell by the way he stood and walked that he was a veteran. What he was saying sounded good, but the phrasing made it seem like you could take it many ways, so Apocrypha reserved judgment. Her past gave her ample reason not to trust agents of The Word.

"Thanks, and you are...?"

"I am Job." He made no indication that he was going to continue.

The name also gave her pause. Sword bringers sometimes took on a new name when they entered the service, but usually, it was something like David or Samson to symbolize becoming a warrior.

"Well, Job, I appreciate you looking out for me, but I am surprised to see a friendly face. I thought the sword bringers pulled out to the suburbs after Chicago was lost."

"I am not a friendly face, just someone who takes his vows seriously. You will need more than that knife to get out of the city alive." He pulled one of his pistols and dropped it to the ground. "Take that and get yourself out of here. I have more to do than keep a tourist out of trouble."

"I'm no tourist. Thanks for the help, but who are you to tell me to scurry along? I have a job to do."

"I am the only law that still resides in this city. I don't know why you are here, but you are outnumbered and outclassed. Go home."

"I am not going anywhere. I have business with a certain Thanatos executive, and I am not leaving till it's concluded."

At the mention of Thanatos, Job cocked his head to the side, suddenly highly interested. "What business is that?"

"I do not have time to tell you the whole story. But Thanatos kidnapped a scientist to try and combine magic and tech and I am here to retrieve him. As well as delivering a well-deserved ass-kicking to the people involved."

Job's face became grim, and he pointed at the gun. "I repeat, take the gun and get out of here. I will handle that." He turned and started sprinting, then dodged into an alley and disappeared.

Apocrypha was only a couple of steps behind him, but when she turned the corner, he was gone.

"Son of a bitch. I hate that ninja crap." She strode slowly back and retrieved the pistol. It was a Vatican Arms forty-five adjudicator. She checked the chamber and slid the gun into the back of her pants.

"Hey, Job, that motherfucker is mine. Stay away from him." She knew Job probably could not hear her, but the yelling helped her vent some frustration. She had been on ops before that had competing operatives on them and they always ended badly. She took a moment to orient herself then headed north.

*

After about two hours, she found herself in Winnetka. It had been one of the wealthiest places in Chicago, so of course, a Corp like Walton would have moved in here. This area was free of ghouls, and she made quick time getting to his residence. The area around it was lit by streetlights that glowed with an unsettling greenish hue.

The house was large and would have reeked of money when there were people in Chicago. It was also surrounded by a group of undead. Apocrypha looked closer. These were not ghouls as she might have hoped; they were more cauldron-born, which meant tougher and smarter. There were about twenty of them, clad in tactical armor and holding automatic weapons like they knew how to use them.

"Well, shit, there is something you don't see every day." She crept back down the street before the cauldron-born had a chance to spot her. She leaned against the wall of a house that seemed to be deserted. Her mind flipped through different scenarios. All of them ended up with her being dead. She pulled out her cell phone and called Kitsune.

She picked up on the first ring. "Hey, partner."

"What are you doing with your phone? I'm going to kill Badb."

"Hey, ease up. As much as I might want to see the two of you end up in a catfight, she is not to blame. Solstice gave my healing a boost, so I'm doing a lot better than I was. I was just wearing my headset in case you happened to call."

"I was going to leave you a voicemail."

"Well, you got the real me, aren't you lucky."

"Okay, well, things are going really well. I will be taking the bad guy out in about ten minutes and then be on my way back home. Nothing for you to worry about."

"Wow, when did you become such a bad liar? Was it when you kissed me?"

Apocrypha held the phone away from her face and tightened her hold on her emotions. "I'm not lying. I'm only tired from kicking all this ass."

"If you lie to me and then die, I will never forgive you."

"Okay, I am facing a little more opposition than I anticipated, and I wanted to hear your voice."

"Give me the details, and maybe I can send you some help."

"I got about twenty heavily armed undead operatives."

"Hmm, can you give me two hours?"

"What are you planning? Am I going to hate it?"

"Oh yeah. You are going to hate it."

"What are you thinking."

"ffff fffff ffff I am going into a tunnel and losing you." Kitsune hung up.

Apocrypha immediately hit redial. It went straight to voicemail. She tried several more times, but Kitsune never picked up.

"When I get my hands on her..."

Apocrypha pulled deeper back into the shadows. She had no choice but to wait now. Rats the size of small dogs scattered as she settled in, then she heard something even larger pounce on them. She hoped that meal would keep whatever it was full while she waited.

After a couple of hours, she heard the screeching of a Cherub, The Word's preferred troop transport, as it descended onto the street with all its guns blazing. The Cherub looked a little the worse for wear. She figured it must have run into some Vrykolakas on the way in.

"What the fuck."

Apocrypha did not know whether to curse Kitsune or praise her. One of the few things that could have broken the siege was a transport full of sword bringers but the only way they would have come this far into Chicago was if Kitsune had told them what she was. The transport made another pass and several of the cauldron-born were cut down. The Cherub landed at the end of the street and the cauldron-born immediately charged them. Apocrypha dashed for the Corp house now that her way was clear. She did not want to risk anyone deciding that she might be worth some ammo, so she did not stop moving when she got to the house, instead diving through one of the windows and rolling as she hit the floor. She came up with the borrowed adjudicator in her hands.

The room inside was almost silent except for the sound of dripping echoing in the room. Every surface was covered in blood. There had apparently been a large contingent of human helpers guarding the interior of the building, and their body parts were now strewn across the floor. Apocrypha wished that her dual nature did not give her excellent night vision. It was evident someone had gotten to the house before her. The person had been able to get past the cauldron-born without raising the alarm but had apparently stopped and taken their time with the humans present.

"Job…" She whispered his name. She could not believe that a sword bringer could do this. Her mind would not accept that, no matter how much she hated The Word. They were bastards but rarely bloodthirsty. Whoever had come through had enjoyed this. It must have been a rival mafia family.

The blood trail led through the kitchen and down into the basement. As she entered the basement, she could see part of the wall had been knocked down, revealing a large cavern that apparently predated the house by some time.

She walked down the passageways. They were old, maybe from prohibition or before, but also with fiber optic cables running through them. Someone had obviously been doing some upgrading lately. Up ahead of her, she could hear talking, and she pulled the hammer back on the forty-five. She crept up to a corner and peered around. There was a large room filled with machinery, and in the middle was a man in a hospital bed. As Apocrypha watched, he grabbed a small device with his mouth and raised the bed to face Job. He looked vaguely like the description of Mr. Walton, but he appeared to have seen better days.

Job stood near the bed with Corey Givens, the scientist Apocrypha had spent so much time trying to find. He had his helmet off and a sword to the throat of Givens. She stepped out from the stairwell. She walked slowly and swiveled her gun to train it on Mr. Walton then Job in turn.

"Nobody fucking do anything. Givens, we need to stop meeting like this. You okay?"

The scientist started to shake his head no but then rethought the action. "I'm alive."

Job turned to look at Apocrypha, and the light caught on his fangs. He was a vampire. Well, that explained why he could not enter the church, but how did a sword bringer become a vampire? Apocrypha walked to the center of the room, trying to work out who she should put a bullet in first. Before she could decide, Walton spoke up.

"You must think me to be an extremely dangerous paraplegic to hold a gun on me?" As he spoke, he smiled openly like a kid at Christmas, displaying his fangs.

"All vampires are dangerous, even ones that appear confined to a hospital bed."

"Oh, I am quite paralyzed. Father Johansson saw to that. That is why I have such an interest in Mr. Givens. Maybe you can talk some sense into the priest, and we can come to an accommodation."

Well, that answered some of Apocrypha's questions. Father Johansson was a bit of a legend; he had refused to leave when given the order to pull out of the urban sections of Chicago. It had been years since anyone had heard from him, and he had been presumed dead. Apparently, the reports had been both right and wrong. She shifted her position slightly so that she could keep everyone in her sight at the same time.

"The filth speaks the truth. Pride goes before the fall, and so it was with me. But I have not allowed my current state to alter my vows to God and the order. I am content to know in the end, I will be redeemed."

"Ah, so that explains the whole Job thing, but not while you are about to kill an innocent person. That hardly seems a way to maintain your oath to the sword bringers."

At her mention of him, Givens started to speak again, but Job tightened his grip, and the sword pressed into his skin, drawing a single drop of blood. Givens sank back into passivity. Job continued as if the person he held was immaterial.

"No one who works for a corp is innocent, but I would slay a hundred innocents if it kept them from restoring Walton to his former self. I worked too hard to gain the vengeance I have wrought on this monster."

"I was not a vampire until you turned me."

"I merely let your outward form mirror your inner self. Mr. Walton was not a bad person. He was a worse person who allowed others to do bad. His machinations enabled the underworld to clean its money from drug deals and protection rackets and even helped them procure innocents for those Dons who believed that virgin blood gave them more power. Then, he chose to retire here when law enforcement began to come after him. He had escaped them, but I vowed he would not escape judgment. I took his hands and feet, then snapped his spine. As he lay dying, I transformed him into one of the undead so that his misery would last forever."

It was an interesting idea. Once you became a vampire, regeneration was part and parcel of the deal, but you had to keep any problems you had prior to the change. Apocrypha admired Job's sense of justice, but she could not let him harm the scientist.

"Then Walton heard of Mr. Givens and discovered that by using new technology, he might be able to find a way to allow magical and supernatural entities to interact with cybernetic limbs and other constructs. I cannot allow him to give movement back to this beast."

"I can see your point, but we can't go around killing everyone who has some innovative technology that a bad guy might use."

"Why not? What has technology ever done but taken us farther from God?"

"Listen, corporations suck. I get that, but there has to be a difference between us and the bad guys. Once we start killing people because they are inconvenient, we cross that line. How about we just put a bullet in Mr. Walton, and I take my leave with Givens."

"He has not suffered long enough."

This was not going to go well, Apocrypha could see. She began to think up her next argument because young, untrained vampires had scary speed and strength. She had no idea what a person with Special Forces-level training could do with it. Out of the corner of her eye, she saw Walton moving his teeth on his remote control. She turned, giving him her full attention.

"What did you just do?"

"I merely wanted to introduce you to my first attempts at fixing my condition. I thought that necromancy might let me attach new body parts to give me back movement. I was unsuccessful, but the results were, shall we say, interesting."

The sound of running feet drew her attention to a group of cells in the back of the room that had been hidden in darkness. Apocrypha shifted, moving parallel with Job so she could see what was coming at them. There was a rush of bodies, but there was something off about them. As they got closer, she realized that all of them had some sort of extra appendage; there were people with four arms, some with three legs, some with arms jutting from their back. They were all also screaming incoherently. Whatever process they had endured to have the limbs attached had also driven them mad with pain. She looked deep into their eyes and realized there was nothing inside but insanity and agony.

The only way to help them was to put them out of their misery. Job obviously felt the same way, but she was not sure he had taken the time to consider what they might have been once. He cast Givens aside immediately and brought his sword up. Then the creatures were upon them. Apocrypha fired into the mass, every shot dropping a body, but there were more than she had bullets for. When the gun clicked empty, she dropped it and pulled out Thorn. The blade glowed silver, confirming their necromantic taint. She swept into the horde. The creatures seemed to be consumed with blood lust but lacked any strength other than that of numbers. Job and Apocrypha made short work of them.

As the last one fell, the earth shook, and a blur of movement surged from the darkness. Apocrypha instinctively threw herself down and to her right. A large fist crashed down where she had been. She was prone on her back, looking up at the monster that confronted her when she had first recovered Givens. It looked like they had added more bodies to repair the damage the fall had caused, and it was truly nauseating.

Bile rose in her throat, and she was overcome by horror for a moment. The giant took that moment to grab Apocrypha with its two large appendages and pull her toward its natural head. As it did so, a slew of other hands raked her body, clawing and scratching as she was dragged over them. Job leaped into action, slashing the ogre with his sword, and it reacted in pain, dropping Apocrypha. It bellowed in blind rage and swatted him, sending him flying into the far wall.

As Apocrypha regained her feet, an icy calm came over her. She had never believed in faith or destiny but somehow felt that her path had taken her to this moment to remove this beast from the earth and release the souls of the people held captive by the power of necromancy. Her dagger shone with a brightness that blinded all those around her. The ogre made a mad rush at her, and she made no move to avoid the attack. When the ogre impacted her, she allowed it to engulf her. She drove her knife deep into its body, pushing farther and farther till it reached its true heart. There was a tremendous thunderclap and an explosion of force, and white light surged out from the heart, filling the chamber. When it was over, Apocrypha was laid out on the floor, and all the bodies had been separated into their individual people. The ogre lay dead. Everything she had worn and carried was gone except for Thorn. She felt almost entirely spent as she rose to her feet and made no effort to cover herself.

Job ran to her side and dropped to his knees. "My angelo rinnegato, you have been given wings."

"Wild angel, what the fuck are you talking about?" Apocrypha looked over her shoulder and Job held his blade to the ground and his head down like he was praying to a shrine. His blade was clean even after all the death it had dealt, and she could see a reflection of her back. There were now two stylized wings that appeared to have been tattooed, covering her shoulder blades to her lower back. She had no idea what any of that meant. She took a few unsteady steps toward Givens. He was unconscious but otherwise seemed none the worse for wear. She started to bend down to pick him up.

Job was there before she could get a hold of him. She prepared herself for another conflict, but he merely handed her his duster, then bent down and picked up Givens.

Apocrypha turned to Walton; after seeing what he had done to these people, she understood what had driven the sword bringer. She was starting to agree with Job that a quick death might be too good for him. Before she could fully formulate what she was going to do, a small rock fell from the ceiling onto her head, then another. The explosion that had resulted from the death of the monstrosity had apparently had a destabilizing effect on the chamber they were in.

She looked upward. "Oh, so you got this, huh?" She glanced over at Job. "We have to go." Once again, Job just nodded his assent and took off down the passageway with Givens over his shoulder in a fireman's carry.

They made it into the above-ground portion of the house a moment before the tunnel collapsed entirely. The house shifted on its foundation and threw them off balance as they exited the front door. As the trio made their way to the street, Apocrypha could see the sword bringers cleaning up the last remains of the cauldron-born in the front yard. Apocrypha's heart froze as she saw that the leader of the group was Roger. She would not have thought he would have come here personally to take her into custody.

"Kit, what did you do?" She sat down resigned. She did not have another fight in her. She looked at Job and struggled for something witty to say but nothing came.

"I guess I will see you next time I come back to Chicago." The comment seemed lame even to herself, but she did not really care.

Job placed Givens gently on the street next to her. "They need a prize. I will give them myself. A vampire priest is not as good as an angelo rinnegato, but it should be enough to keep them occupied for a while."

He raised his hands and called to the troops of The Word. The sword bringers leveled their guns at him and froze. Father Johansson had been a legend and seeing him back out of the blue surprised them.

Roger alone looked past Job to where Apocrypha sat. He told his men to get Job on board the Cherub and walked directly toward her.

She pulled the duster around her more tightly as he approached.

He reached out a hand to help her up. "Come with me if you want to live."

Apocrypha forced a smile, but it did not reach her eyes. She knew he was trying to lighten the mood, but she was not feeling it. "So now what? You take me to be judged?"

"No, I just give you and your friend a ride home. I can tell my boss that I was advised about Father Johannson still walking around and I came to get him. The unit is loyal to me and won't say anything unless directly questioned. Father Johansson, I am sure, will be the only topic of conversation for quite some time. It does mean I will have to hit up Father Raphael for confession about the lie. You know he was the one who told me I should meet you in the first place."

"Really, well, that explains some things. Are you sure, though? I mean, you don't really know me, and the archbishop would love to have me under his thumb."

"I could say I am a good guy, but you might not buy that. What I can say is that my allegiance at the end of the day is to the Lord and not to an officer of the church, and I think He has more plans for you."

Apocrypha raised an eyebrow.

"Also, a certain hacker promised unholy vengeance and the publication of my internet history if I broke my promises."

Apocrypha actually chuckled at that. Roger put his hand out again, and she took it, letting him pull her to her feet.

Epilogue

Apocrypha was in the hospital again. This time was different, though the beeping of the machine was drowned out by the low chanting of the street shaman. A soft light illuminated the body of her father. She had been surprised that Vince had come through with the full payment for the mission. Apocrypha had been sure he would try to weasel out. The fact they had established a relationship with the Dagda Corporation, which let him add International to the Sin Eaters brand, probably convinced him.

She leaned her head back to stretch her neck but immediately snapped to attention when her father started groaning. She surged out of the chair but stopped as the shaman raised his hand.

"It will pass."

"It better."

If the shaman had heard Apocrypha, he gave no indication but merely kept on chanting. After a moment, sweat broke out on his head, and he made a series of intricate gestures with his hands.

A moment later, the light surrounding her father exploded in brilliance. Her father sat bolt upright, screaming, then collapsed back on the bed.

Apocrypha was across the room in a heartbeat. She had grabbed the shaman by the collar and lifted him into the air with one hand before she had time to think. "What the hell did you do?"

"Ack."

Before Apocrypha could take further action, a loud snore came from her father. She released her grip, and the shaman hit the ground with a thud.

"He is out of the coma but will probably sleep for the rest of the day. The disease held a tight grip and did not want to be purged."

"Sorry."

"It happens more times than you would expect."

"Maybe, but it was unprofessional. I will send you an extra tip." Apocrypha pulled out her phone to send Sanders the payment.

"Not needed, just spread the word about my services. He should be better with rest and food. If anything comes up, you have my number." Sanders's phone binged as the payment went through. He gave it a quick look then got to his feet and walked out of the room without another word. Apocrypha tentatively reached out and touched her father's hand. It was warm.

"Hey, Dad, guess you're going to be okay." She pulled the chair next to his bedside and did not move for three hours.

She gave his hand a final squeeze and got to her feet. She walked out to the nurses' desk. "Hey, do you have a pen and a piece of paper I could use?"

"Yeah, sure."

Apocrypha took a moment; this was probably the hardest

thing she had ever done. She steeled herself. This had to be done to keep everybody safe. She scribbled a note and folded it in half. She walked back into her dad's room and laid it on the table next to him, where she hoped he would see it as soon as he woke. Then she pulled out her phone and dialed Kitsune.

Kitsune answered on the first ring. "Hey, partner."

"Hey, Kit. How are you doing." Apocrypha closed her eyes to shut out her emotions.

"I'm doing well. A combination of elven magic and honorary Dagda Corp health care benefits means I should be out of here in a couple of days. How's your dad?"

"He's going to be okay. The shaman cleansed the disease. Now he just needs rest."

"That's awesome." Kitsune squealed. "Oh, I have more good news. Nuada took off, but he left a present behind. A bag of gold coins. I have no idea what an ancient Celtic coin is worth, but it's got to be a lot, right?"

"Probably. That reminds me, is there any way we might be able to get Givens and Nuada in contact with one another? He might be able to help the Fae with that whole one-arm thing."

"I can do that."

"Cool. I mean, I am not Nuada's biggest fan but anything that screws Tethra makes my day a little brighter. I also need a personal favor. Are you able to do your keyboard magic yet?"

"Absolutely. What do you need?"

"I need you to zero my dad. I need all his electronic records purged and set him up with a new identity. Then, take half of whatever you get from the coins and throw it into a bank account. An actual bank account, not one of those cryptocurrencies things you are always talking about."

"Sure, I can do that. As soon as I get off the phone, I'll start.

Should be up and running except for the bank account in about an hour."

"Great, one more thing I owe you for."

"You worried about The Word coming after him?"

"Yeah, just a matter of time till Job talks about me and what he saw. They are going to be hellbent on coming after me and my family."

"That sucks. Well, I will take care of everything for him. Then, when I get back in town, we can find a cozy place to snuggle and figure out how we can avoid them."

"That sounds like a plan. Bye, partner." Apocrypha hung up. One thing she had never learned to do was lie easily and that one had hurt a lot. The next call she was kind of looking forward to.

"Sin Eaters International, how can we be of service."

"Hey Marie, can I talk to Vince."

"He's...umm...not available at the moment."

"Okay, just tell him I called to say I quit. Bye." Apocrypha hung up. Three seconds later, her phone started ringing. A slow smile played across her face as she pushed to have her phone block that number. Then she pulled up her list of contacts and found Roger's number. The phone rang several times before he picked up.

"Oh, hey, it's you. Listen, it's not a great time. Let me call you back from a different number."

"Nope, I need to talk to you right away, and yes, I know your calls are monitored for better customer service and all that bull-shit. I wanted to say thanks again for saving my ass. Oh, by the way, what did everybody think of Job?"

"They are trying to figure out what to do with him. It's not every day a decorated commander comes back from the dead."

"I could see that. Well, the reason for my call is that I figured since you were nice enough to give me a ride home, I should share some things."

Roger interrupted her. "You really don't need to."

"No, I do. You know I am not your average freelance corporate asset. I am a God damn Nephilim. By the way, the pun was intended for those listening in. I am a child of the fallen. The kind of person the church has been hunting for various reasons for millennia, and you all almost had me. But I am leaving the city now, heading for Europe, actually, and you are all welcome to come and try to claim me there. But come loaded for bear cuz I will be waiting for you."

"Shit."

"Yeah... I know I just made your life a lot more interesting; my apologies."

Apocrypha hung up and dropped the phone. A moment later, she brought her foot down on it, smashing it to bits. She reached down and pulled off her gun belt and holster, then walked over to the magical waste disposal bin in the corner of the room. She dropped all her armaments except Thorn and her purse into the bin before hitting the purge button. The entire contents would be incinerated with white-hot fire, and she was confident nothing would be left.

She grabbed the sleeves of her hoodie sweatshirt and concentrated, remembering the black lacy dress from the night in Ireland. The clothing was shimmed and reshaped, and she walked out of the hospital with her head held high. First on to the Gate, then off to London. She hoped Crossroads still had job openings available.

Acknowledgements

To Kathy, Rich, and all the other beta readers who gave me their input. Thanks to Steve and John, I appreciate your inspiration.

About the Author

Kathryne Lentes has been writing stories as long as she could hold a pen in her hand. She is a transwoman who, when not working on her own projects, operates Paper Phoenix Ink, a blog showcasing queer creators. She is currently living in Saint Louis with her wife, two cats, and a pile of science fiction and fantasy books.

Email
Kathryne.lentes@paperphoenixink.com

Facebook
www.facebook.com/kathryne.lentes

X
@paperphoenixink

Website
www.paperphoenixink.com

Other NineStar books by this author

The Night Menagerie

CONNECT WITH NINESTAR PRESS

WEBSITE: NINESTARPRESS.COM

FACEBOOK: NINESTARPRESS

X: @NINESTARPRESS

INSTAGRAM: NINESTARPRESS

BLUESKY: NINESTARPRESS

THREADS: @NINESTARPRESS

www.ingramcontent.com/pod-product-compliance
Lightning Source LLC
Chambersburg PA
CBHW070536100726
47907CB00004B/1136